SWORD

OF

ELFAME

BOOK ONE:
BEYOND THE SHORES
OF TIME

by

Larry C. Hedrick

TOP OF THE MOUNTAIN PUBLISHING
Largo, Florida 34643-5117 U.S.A.

Top Of The Mountain Publishing
11701 South Belcher Road, Suite 123
Largo, Florida 34643-5117 U.S.A.
SAN 287-590X
FAX (813) 536-3681
PHONE (813) 530-0110

Library of Congress Cataloging Publication Data
Hedrick, Larry C.
Sword of elfame / by Larry C. Hedrick.
p. cm.
Summary: Nikki Renn is drawn into a battle with the archdemon Apollyon, only to find that she and her companions are responsible for the fate of every soul of the human race.
ISBN 1-56087-021-4 : $9.95
[1. Fantasy.]   I. Title.
PZ7.H3564Sw   1991
[Fic] -dc 20   91-35051 CIP AC

Cover and interior art by Stan Morrison

Manufactured in the United States of America

DEDICATION

I would like to dedicate this book to my wife Sonya, who has been the greatest help to me in its writing. Not only has she believed in me when so many others offered only discouragement, but she is also one of the greatest editors one could ever have.

Larry C. Hedrick

PRONUNCIATION GAZETTEER

(Based upon Gaelic and Welsh)

Cait Sidth.... (Cait Shee)

Ciuthach.... (Kew-uch)

Fir Darrig.... (Fir Yaraga)

Fin Bheara.... (Fin-Vara)

Firbolgs.... (Fir Vulag)

Gwragedd Annwn.... (Gwrageth Anoon)

Gwartheg Y Llyn.... (Gwarrtheg er thlin)

Gwydion.... (Gwideeon)

Gwyn ap Nudd.... (Gwin ap Neethe)

Ossian.... (Isheen)

Phouka.... (Pooka)

Sithein.... (Sheean)

Tir nan Og.... (Teer na nogue)

Tuatha de Danann.... (Tootha day Danan)

Tylwyth Teg.... (Terlooeth Teig)

CONTENTS

ILLUSTRATIONS

CHAPTER I

Music of the Spheres

$\mathcal{T}$he high-heeled sandals were the sexiest shoes Nikki Renn had come across at the mall last night. They had immediately delighted her with their slender thongs buckling high above her ankles and the delicate way the silver straps caressed her legs. She sat before the full-length mirror in her room, wearing nothing but a very scant purple bikini, and bent down to buckle on the left sandal. Sitting back in her chair, she extended a well-tanned leg, rotating her foot right, then the other.

"All right, now *that's* what I call perfect," she said happily, and then quickly buckled on the other sandal.

The sandals were the ultimate accessory for her new purple bikini, which she had also purchased at the mall the night before. Nikki thought it the ideal outfit for the glamour layout Paul was taking of her, for his summer photography class project. In the privacy of her mind, she thought how exciting it would be if she were to let Paul do the layout with her topless. It was a daring thought, and she was well aware that it was on the border between sexy and vulgar, but she felt she possessed the good taste to pull it off, and to make it work. Still, she had not been able to coax herself into actually talking to him about doing it.

Paul had just begun his college summer quarter and if this project panned out, it would not only net him a top grade but would also provide him with the perfect accent for his portfolio. The portfolio was being prepared for a local magazine, where he hoped to land an intern's job.

Nikki stood and walked to the full-length mirror attached to her closet door. "Very sexy," she whispered as she surveyed her lithe body displayed in a scant T-back. Quickly she added, "but not vulgar!"

Nikki and her friends usually went freely about their beach community in their bathing suits. They went to the burger stands, into shops near the boardwalk, and to the convenience stores of the neighborhood, in their cute but always modest swimsuits without giving it a second thought. Now Nikki would be going about in the T-back bikini giving to everyone its alluring full display of her derriere and its youthful sexuality. She was working hard to convince herself that this was just being progressive, not sluttish.

Unlike her private dreams of posing topless for Paul's photography project, she had actually brought herself to buy the bikini, with the very intent of making a public display of herself, of really arousing the guys when she wore it. She had convinced herself at the mall that it did not go over that border and make her look lewd, and now she worked hard to reinforce that thought.

Nikki's friends often complemented her on looking like an 18-year-old version of Michelle Pfeiffer, and she had to admit (although never publicly) that she did her best to enhance that look. She struck a few poses for the mirror, trying her Marilyn vamp-look, and striking a very sultry Raquel Welch pose.

"Damn, I look good!" she said, watching her reflection give back a well-practiced version of the look — that slinky, sultry pout that rocketed Sophia Loren to fame. Nikki, wrapped in a glow of self-appreciation, reached for the closet door and pulled it open to get her beach jacket.

She screamed as a flurry of snow-white fur hit her squarely in the face. Her arms fought the air, and she fell backward onto the carpeted floor in front of the opened closet. A sharp pain streaked her left cheek before the choking cloud of furry white bounded clear of her with a hiss.

She rolled to her knees, trembling from the sudden shock. She felt a warm trickle on her cheek. "*World War Three!*" She fought back tears brought on by the sting of the cat's scratch on her cheek.

The enormous white cat, which had bounded into her face from the top shelf of her closet, now bowed and spat at her from the middle of her bed. She had nicknamed the cat *World War Three*, not knowing his real name, but saying that everywhere he went turned into a war zone. And he always seemed to turn up in the oddest places!

"What the devil were you doing in my closet? And why can't you stay next door where you belong, you stupid cat?" She got up trembling and walked back to the mirror to inspect her face.

In the meantime, *World War Three* busily bathed himself on Nikki's bed as if his contact with Nikki had defiled his silky fur.

"Great. Really great!" she pouted, looking into the mirror and blotting the scratch with a tissue. "This is going to ruin my photo session with Paul," Nikki stormed. "Hmm, maybe a little makeup will hide it."

She returned her attention to the cat. "And now, your Royal Highness of Pussdom!" The cat perked up to look at her. "You are about to have your regal self cast out!"

The cat meowed his displeasure loudly, as she picked him up and tossed him out an open window onto the porch roof just below.

"And stay out!" she shouted after him, mumbling to herself, "Fat chance of that. He'll be back first time he sees the window open!" Unconsciously she reached up to re-tie the thin strap around her neck. It had begun to come loose during the cat fight and now her top threatened to come completely off.

World War Three belonged to Old Joshua next door. Old Joshua was the neighborhood enigma — the kind of old person that children love to puzzle over and to terrify themselves with. No one knew much about the old man, except that he had lived in his old house for more years than anyone cared to count. Neither could anyone figure out his strange white cat, who at one time or another had turned up in every pantry, cupboard and closet on the block.

Folks rarely spoke to the old man, nor he to them, as he spent most of his time closed up in his towering old Victorian house with stained glass windows. When he did speak he always seemed civil enough, but still Nikki got a creepy feeling whenever she saw him, almost as if the old man could read the deepest secrets of her mind.

From her upper window she could easily see over the high hedgerow between her house and Joshua's. As she tossed the cat out the window, she caught sight of the old man standing in his yard. Old Joshua stooped to pluck *World War Three* from the ground as the oversized white cat strolled home; he looked up at her just as she was re-tying her bikini top. Her face flushed with embarrassment and suddenly she felt very naked in front of the old man.

"Good morning, Nikki," spoke Old Joshua as he looked up at her. "Remember when Mister *Dumpty* fell from the wall? All the king's horses and all the king's men couldn't put *Humpty* together again. Let's hope our glue is better than theirs was my dear, what?"

Then, with a wry smile, he said something else unintelligible about 'gryphons never lying.' With that the old man turned and walked into his huge Victorian house, scratching his cat behind the ears. Nikki stared after him a moment in puzzlement before her mind clicked to the time.

"Oh, for goodness sake, now I'm late for Paul's!" She grabbed her sheer beach jacket from the closet rack, tossed it over her shoulders and made for the door.

In the hall she nearly bought a free ride down the stairs on her brother's skateboard. Often, as now, she wondered what brothers were for if not to be a constant threat to the life and sanity of their sisters.

"Hey, come back with my skateboard!" her 15-year-old brother, had materialized in the doorway next to Nikki's room.

"You know you could have killed me leaving this thing here," shouted Nikki as she spun toward the boy. She then gave the skateboard a kick which sent it careening down the hallway and through the upstairs bathroom door where it banged to a stop against the tub.

"Watch it!" the boy shouted and ran to cradle the maligned possession. "I'll tell Dad you're going to see Pauley with no clothes on." This came with a particularly well-practiced younger brother's smirk as he returned from the bathroom carrying the skateboard.

"No, you won't, you little rat," Nikki returned as she descended the stairs. "Besides, Daddy is downstairs now and we talked over my buying this swimsuit last night. It's perfectly decent."

"Yeah, for a nudist colony. Your whole butt's showing," Harold sniped, then quickly ducked back into the same door he had appeared from, just missing contact from a well-aimed rubber ball left on the stairs and now being launched by his sister's hand.

Nikki bounded down the stairs and out the door. The high heels of her sandals made a rap-tap sound as she clopped purposefully up the sidewalk toward Paul's house three blocks away.

An orange VW with the top down wheeled around the corner and headed toward Nikki. Two guys were sitting up on the back of the rear seat, two girls in the seat between their feet. Another girl sat in the front beside the driver, a third guy.

"Hey Nikki," redheaded Allison squealed, "I can't believe you had the nerve to really do it. I love it!" The others waved vigorously.

Two of the guys whistled and wolf-called. "Far out!" one of them cried. "That's the way to strut it Nikki, show 'em something they'll never forget!"

"I've got to get Erin into one of those numbers," the other boy called.

Each of the guys received hearty elbow jabs and smacks from the young ladies between their feet.

"The beach is this way!" shouted one of the blondes in the back seat. It was Sandy, Allison's cousin.

"But Paul's isn't!" called Sandy's sister, Erin. The three girls were Nikki's best friends. It was Allison who had first seen the bikini on the mall mannequin and it was this quartet who had hatched the plot of Nikki's posing in such scant attire for Paul's photo study.

"Lucky Paul!" Erin's boyfriend shouted. Erin threw him another elbow jab as the car putt-putted down the street; Nikki laughed and waved after it.

As she continued up the street, the smells of a fresh new summer brought back memories of the past year. It was on a summer's day much like this when she had moved from Chicago to South Shores,

Florida, and met Paul. He had been one of the first people to appear at their two-story Tudor house when the she and her family had driven up behind the moving van.

Nikki loved that house, especially the great backyard with its cherry trees surrounding a white gazebo and its split-rail fence around the yard.

Across the split-rail fence and directly behind their house was an empty lot with a solitary giant sycamore tree growing right in its center. Nikki often wondered why no one had ever cut it down to build a house. Maybe the reason was that no one had the heart to kill something that had survived for so long. Whatever the reason, Nikki was glad the fine old tree had endured. Children for blocks around came to play in the lot beneath the shade tree and sometimes it seemed every bird in the county nested in its branches.

Paul had turned out to be an absent-minded young man, maybe even a touch eccentric, but Nikki felt a good artist was supposed to be just a tad unusual. Paul had explained to Nikki that following graduation he would work for a magazine for a few years. That way he could save up enough money to open his own photography studio. Of course, Nikki had altered those plans just enough to include herself, but she had not yet let Paul in on the secret of exactly where and when he would propose to her.

Nikki popped back to reality when she realized she was ringing Paul's door bell.

A blondish, rather good looking young man opened the door to the white colonial-styled home. "Oh, that suit is perfect for what I have in mind!" he raved. "Come on in, I'll get the equipment set up."

"Why good morning, Nikki! How lovely you are looking today, Nikki! I do love your new swim suit, Nikki... You think you have it now?" quipped Nikki. "Good, then repeat after me..."

"What?" Paul turned from rummaging through a cedar chest filled with camera equipment. "Oh, yes, I'm sorry. You look very nice. Here, help me get this back-drop in place."

With an exasperated sigh, Nikki helped Paul transform the living room of his father's home into a photography studio.

"Do something with these." Paul handed an armful of trophies to Nikki. His father was Coach Martin, the head football coach at the local high school. He had never quite understood why Paul would rather take pictures of games than play in them, but after many years arguing over the subject it had finally been laid to rest.

The room was finished and Nikki had just laid her jacket to one side when Paul walked up to her and placed his hands on her bare hips.

"Now, what were you saying when you came in?" He slid his hands around to encircle her waist.

"You know good and well what I was saying, but now that you mention it..." She drew him close to her and gave him a long, deep kiss, then pulled back. "Now, we're supposed to be taking pictures today, remember?"

"Ah, yeah, right." Paul, somewhat reluctantly, tore his attention from Nikki and finished setting up his tripod while she loosened up for posing.

"How do you like the bikini?" she asked him when his attention finally returned to her.

"Off," he quipped.

"Oh, yeah?" Nikki drew herself up into her best Pfeiffer "look" as she lifted her arms above her head, tossed her hair back, and reached behind her neck, pulling herself into a sensuous stretch.

"Go ahead, take your best shot, this is as close as it gets," she intoned in a sultry voice.

"Oh man, that's great!" Paul was beside himself as he worked the camera. "Now just hold it for one more second and..."

The strobe of Paul's camera flashed and the world suddenly came to an end.

* * *

Blind terror flooded Nikki's mind as the universe exploded, blasting outward with the power of a billion dying galaxies. Nikki watched as reality dissolved into the blackness of an eternal void. She felt herself drifting into nothingness, but at the same time she also felt a sinister presence; the mind of a vastly evil creature which reached out briefly to touch her. It was as if the creature gloated in the face of its mortal enemy — and Nikki knew that somehow she was that creature's mortal enemy.

A wave of nausea swept over her and she thought she was going to heave her insides out. How could she though, when her stomach didn't even seem to be a part of her body anymore?

Suddenly, seemingly from a million miles away, she felt a hand grasp hers. Recognizing it as Paul's, she fought to hold back the panic which threatened to take over her brain, wherever her brain was. All her senses were going haywire. Then there was the music... kind of like music, but was more the sound of a thousand idiot flute players blasting a psychotic nightmare symphony.

The lunatic sound ate deep into her soul as it grew and grew within her head.

"Oh my God, Paul. Pauley where are you!" She felt the hand slip from her grasp. The maddening symphony of the flutes worked itself into her mind, threatening to rip her spirit into oblivion.

Then began the other music. It started lightly in the corner of her mind, a universe away from the screaming madness of the wild flutes. The soft music rose until finally it could compete with the crazy fluting. Nikki's mind began to calm. It occurred to her that the voices of everything in creation had at once joined in one great choir. Everything from the greatest star to the smallest sub-atomic particle seemed to sing out until the music filled her being. She felt her body and being coming together again.

✳ ✳ ✳

Everything around her was black. Not dark, there was light, everything was just black. The jet floor beneath her shown as a polished mirror with a light which came from nowhere. Nikki took a few steps, and the sound of her sandals echoed forever. It was then she realized there were no walls around her, just the blackness of an eternal space without stars.

"Nikki!" a voice called from somewhere far away.

"Pauley, is that you? Over here! Where are you?" Nikki called back.

In a moment she heard the patting of sneakers and Paul appeared from her right, out of the eternal blackness.

"This is rather strange, isn't it? Don't you think so?" Paul asked.

"Strange? Pauley, where are we?" She was fighting to keep the panic from taking over again. For a moment she thought she heard the mad flutes resuming. "Have I gone crazy? What's happening to us?"

She grabbed for him, locked her arms around him, felt his arms wrap around her waist, the material of his tank top pressing against the bareness of her stomach.

"We're okay, honey, we're all right," he tried to soothe her. She was by now choking to hold back sobs. "I think they overcame them, drove them off."

"What, who do you mean?" she asked, drawing back just far enough to be able to look into his blue eyes.

"The singers," he returned. "I think they drove off the mad flute players."

"Then... you heard the strange music? I thought I was going crazy."

"Then we both are, because I heard it, too. No, whatever it was, it was real and it happened to us both."

"Not quite real, my children," a voice boomed around them; powerful, yet not frightening. There was a strange comfort in the strength of that voice.

The two looked up, and saw the speaker towering above them like a colossus from a long forgotten age.

"Apollyon could never be described as quite real — rather he is the essence of all that never should have been, yet was."

"Who are you?" Paul seemed to be in possession of the situation.

I guess it pays to be a bit eccentric, Nikki thought as Paul spoke, because when things begin to go crazy, you can sort of meet them halfway.

Paul continued, "And what's happened to me and Nikki?"

"I am Erion of Those-Who-Serve, the All-Council of El Elyon, the Father Creator," the colossus replied. "You have been snatched from the fist of Apollyon by the *music of the spheres*. We almost lost you, for the music of the spheres was dying as Apollyon grew in power."

"We had hoped to come to you before Apollyon located you," the colossus continued. "For lo these many years we have kept you hidden and then, just as we were about to call upon you, you were discovered and all was nearly lost."

Things were happening too fast and had gone too far for Nikki.

"I want to go home. Now!" she demanded.

"You cannot go back, Nikki Renn."

"How do you know my name?" Erion seemed not to hear Nikki's question.

"You cannot go back to what you once knew, for it no longer exists. With the attack of Apollyon came the end of all that was and ever would have been. Of all that was, only you two were saved, along with three others."

"Paul, I'm scared," Nikki whimpered.

"Silence, child," Erion commanded. Paul hugged her closer to him.

"The time for fear has passed; behold, the time of all things has passed. It is time now to act upon those things that might-have-been in hopes of restoring that which once was!"

CHAPTER II

Things That Might-Have-Been

*N*ikki was sick. She was lying on the floor holding her stomach which cramped and knotted, then slowly eased. The pile of the carpet burned her face as she convulsed with one last cramp.

She sat up as the sickness passed and her vision cleared. Paul sat in the middle of the floor cross-legged. With eyes squinted shut he pinched the bridge of his nose as if to drive away a headache.

"Pauley, are you all right?" Nikki asked, weakly. "What happened? Where's Erion?"

"That sure wasn't a dream," Paul observed as he fixed a pair of gold metal-framed glasses on his face.

Nikki tried standing, her slender legs trembling like those of a newborn filly. "You don't wear glasses. You never have."

"It seems I do now," Paul returned. "When I came to, they were lying on the floor beside me. And things definitely look fuzzy without them."

"Then things aren't what they were," Nikki said.

Paul reached for a leg of the camera tripod to steady himself as he stood up.

"And what did Erion say about time to act now on what might-have-been?" she asked.

"'The time for fear is passed,' he said," Paul replied. "'Behold, the time of all things has passed. It is time now to act upon those things which may have been...'"

"Paul?" a woman's voice called, interrupting his recollection.

The voice became incarnate; a tall, strikingly attractive blond woman stepped into the archway connecting the living room to the house's central hall.

"Why don't you and Nikki take a break and come into the kitchen?" Her bare feet sank into the plush carpet as she stood with thumbs hooked in the belt loops of her short denim cut-offs. She wore a man's white shirt with the tail tied in a knot over her bare midriff.

"I fixed some sandwiches for you and Nikki. Do you want milk or iced tea?" she asked Nikki with a smile.

"Tea," Nikki said. "I, uh..." Nikki could find no other words. The three stood silent for a moment.

"What's the matter with you two?" the woman said, breaking the silence good-naturedly. "You both look as if you'd seen a ghost. Anyhow, the food's on the table if you can un-transfix yourselves!"

She turned with the graceful flow of a professional dancer and disappeared up the hall, her bare feet moving silently on the hall carpet. The two stared after her in amazement.

"Paul, was that..?"

"My mother," he completed her sentence without turning to face Nikki, "...my mother who died of cancer five years ago."

"Pauley?" Nikki's voice began to hold a tremor of panic. "This is getting scary."

"Mother," Paul whispered. Neither had moved since the woman appeared in the archway, but now Paul turned to face Nikki. He adjusted his glasses, which should not have been there.

"We may as well have some lunch while we think this over," Paul said. His voice seemed to calm the panic which fluttered like bat wings within her head.

"I guess so, Paul, but this is unnerving!"

"Of course it is. But I'm also hungry, so let's eat!"

He took her hand and led her up the hall toward the kitchen. On the way they passed the open door of a room lined with mirrors, which also held a rail that ran its length. Paul's mother stood with one leg on the rail working on stretching exercises before the mirrored wall.

Paul paused a moment and watched her. His "mother" saw him and waved to him from the mirror.

"We're going to eat now," he said.

She brought her leg down from the rail, and turned to face the pair. "Fine," she said, wiping perspiration from her forehead. "Clean up after yourselves if you don't mind. I have to be at the studio in a few minutes for my class at one o'clock."

Something in Paul made him want to rush over to this woman and fling his arms around her. It had been five long years since his mother had died. Still, the idea of this world not really being his held him back. If this world was not his, he reasoned, then neither was this mother. This was only how she might-have-been, had that test come back negative.

Paul shook the thoughts from his mind. "Sure, we'll be glad to clean up."

"Oh, Nikki," Paul's mother flashed a bright smile at the girl. "I meant to say something to you about your new bikini. Very stylish, I must say. I've got to try it on when I have a little more time."

"Sure, uh, anytime."

"Well, you two have fun," Mother replied, slipping on a pair of Reeboks. "Take lots of great pictures and I'll see you later." She picked up a tote bag which sat near the door, tossed it over her shoulder, kissed Paul on the forehead, then left through the hall.

Nikki and Paul went on to the kitchen where they found a large plate of sandwiches and a pitcher of iced tea. Nikki had not realized how hungry she was until she had taken the first few bites.

"Hum, not bad for an unreal meal," Paul commented through a mouthful of salami, cheese, lettuce and tomato with mayonnaise and lots of pepper. "Just the way I like it," he added.

Might-have-been sandwiches filled the stomach as adequately as any the two had ever tasted. Before long their hunger was satisfied and they turned back to the problem of rescuing reality from the clutches of an archdemon.

"As I figure it," Paul began, after washing down the last bite of his third sandwich with a large gulp of tea, "Erion sent us here to try to figure out some way Apollyon might-have-been stopped from destroying all creation."

"Then you think if we find out how Apollyon might-have-been stopped, we might be able to help Erion put things back the way they were?" Nikki asked.

"Maybe so." Paul tossed his napkin on the table, pushed his chair back and began pacing the kitchen.

"But Apollyon is supposed to be some kind of devil or something," Nikki mused, "and just how in the world are we supposed to stop something even Erion and his people can't handle?"

"A good point," Paul allowed, as he continued to pace, hands jammed deep into the pockets of his jeans. "They do seem to be a bit more potent than we are, don't they?"

Nikki flopped the half-eaten portion of her second sandwich on her plate. "We don't even know who the other three are who are supposed to help us."

"Of course!" Paul spun around, jabbing a finger at the girl. "That's it! Nikki, you're positively brilliant!"

"What? What did I say?"

"That's why we were sent here! It has to be," the boy said. "The first thing we must do is find the other three that Erion spoke of. And it must be something only we can do or else Erion would have put us all together to begin with. Erion seemed to say that we have some sort of power over Apollyon. I gathered that the Big "A" was scared stiff of us for some reason, so he sent out spies, found me and you, then struck while the iron was hot, so to speak."

"Then what can we do now?" Nikki asked. "We don't even know what it was that could have defeated this Apollyon to begin with. And now with the whole world, everything that existed gone, what can we possibly hope to accomplish even if we find the other three?"

"Oh, I don't think we are doing so badly for now," Paul piped, a wide-eyed, cheerful look on his fair face. "We've already figured out several things that might be on the right track. And considering that the world we're in at present is only one that might-have-been, well, what more could you possibly want for starters?"

Somehow Paul's calm acceptance of this crazy way of looking at things helped Nikki force a feeling somewhat like the wild flapping of bats back into a far corner of her head. For the time being, she was also able to put aside the fact that everything she had ever known no longer existed. She would just latch onto this curly-haired young eccentric who had such a lovable way of facing stark insanity with a face full of cheerful optimism. He would see her through this and back to reality, she reasoned — if there really was a way to get back.

"I'll clean up," Nikki said, pushing back from the table. "You just keep unraveling, Pauley. You're doing great so far."

Paul continued to pace while Nikki's heels made clip-clop sounds across the kitchen tiles as she moved from table to sink. When she had finished cleaning up, she dried her hands and made the half-conscious move of retying her top which had again worked itself loose.

"Just take that off if you want to," Paul teased.

"What are... Oh you!" she blushed, then suddenly shot her hand to her cheek in a flash of remembrance. "It's gone!" she shouted. "The scratch on my face is gone!"

"Yes, it is at that," Paul commented. "I never did get around to asking you what had happened. By the way, how did your face get scratched?"

"That weird cat, *World War Three*, scratched me," Nikki replied. "He had somehow gotten into my closet and this morning when I opened the door he jumped out into my face."

"You never know where that crazy cat is going to pop up. Once I opened my trunk to get a camera and there he was, curled up around my telephoto lens case. Nothing quite like cat fur in your camera," Paul asserted. "Anyway, with all that's happened I don't think you should be so surprised over your scratch being gone. I never wore glasses before an hour ago, remember?"

"It's not that," Nikki retorted. "It's something I remembered just now when I had to re-tie the top of my bikini. You see, after *World War Three* jumped on me I carried him to the window and threw him onto my porch roof, toward Old Joshua's yard."

"And?"

"And I stood there for a minute, you know, to be sure I hadn't hurt him when I threw him out," she said. "I stood there watching the cat stroll back to his house from where he had landed and I could feel blood trickling down my face."

"In the back of my mind I knew my top was coming untied and I began to re-tie the neck strap so I wouldn't fall out, just like a minute ago," she paused for a moment.

Paul nodded for her to continue.

"Well, that's when Old Joshua walked over and picked up the cat. Then the crazy old codger looked up at me. I thought he was just being a dirty old man so I started to say something but he spoke first."

"What did he say?" Paul moved closer to her, intent on her story.

"That's what I thought was so crazy and I didn't even remember it until just a minute ago. He quoted some of *Humpty Dumpty* to me!"

"He what?"

"Honest, he stood there in his yard looking up at me and talked about *Humpty Dumpty*. Then he said something even stranger," she added. "He grinned and said, 'You can believe me because gryphons never lie.'"

"That should certainly give us something more to mull over, shouldn't it?" Paul said, rubbing his chin and giving a stare into space. "Let's go back into the living room where we can be more comfortable."

Paul lead the way and Nikki's sandals clip-clopped across the kitchen floor, hushing as they sank into the deep pile of the hall carpet. Paul paused by the open door to the dance room.

"We changed that into a den three years ago, Dad and I." He walked into the room and Nikki followed.

"There are her awards," he pointed to the far wall where the mirrors ended. "We left those when we made the den." He walked over to the wall and began looking through the photos, ribbons and plaques.

"These are all new," he said, pointing to several on the upper end, "and this one is dated this year." He took one of the pictures from the wall.

"Look, you even took this picture," Nikki said, pointing to Paul's initials in the corner of the photo. It was a custom of his to etch a tiny "P.M." into the lower right corner of all his prints.

A tear fell from his eye to the framed picture. "Why can't this be real and what's gone be the dream?" he said, a sob forming in his throat.

"Oh, why can't *this* be what's real, Nikki?" He dropped the photo and put his arms around her.

His breath came in long jerking sobs as he buried his face in the girl's long brunette hair.

"I thought I was over her dying," he choked out. "For five years I got used to the fact she would never be back and now..." His throat caught, but he continued, "and now I can't even keep her because none of this is the real world!"

For long moments they stood, silently crying in one another's embrace. Finally Paul seemed to get hold of himself. Straightening up, he wiped his eyes, blew his nose on a handkerchief from his pocket.

"Pauley, I'm sorry," Nikki said, sniffling back a tear. "I'm so sorry, what can I do?"

"Oh, I'm okay now," he replied, his voice now seeming to return to normal. "It's just a bit unsteadying to come across one's dead mother after five years. I guess I've missed her more than I have let myself think. Come on, let's get back to the living room. We still have a whale of a lot to work out."

They walked back to the living room where they were just in time to see a great white cat prancing across the room, heading for a posing stool.

"Hey!" Nikki jabbed a finger at *World War Three*, who now bowed and hissed at them from the stool for which he had just claimed ownership.

"Okay, puss, I don't know how you got in here but I sure as heck know how you are going out," Paul said, as he dashed into the room, intent upon nabbing the intruding feline.

Before he could reach the stool the cat, sprang across the corner of the room to the chair where Nikki had laid her beach top.

"Watch those claws," Nikki shouted. "He'll rip that top all to pieces!"

Paul made a grab for the cat who slashed his hand with a lightening slap of his paw. Then the cat grabbed a corner of the beach top in his mouth and bolted from the chair and through the archway to the hall.

"Catch him, he's got my new top!" Nikki shouted.

"Come back here, you furry little thief," Paul shouted as he dove after the fleeing feline. He did a belly flop on the floor just beneath the arch, barely missing the cat, then sprang to his feet and sprinted down the hall, Nikki close on his heels.

"Give me back my new top you filthy little beast!" she shouted as they broke into the kitchen just in time to see *World War Three* hit the back screen door. It swung open with the weight of the cat, allowing him to bolt freely from the house and across the yard, the purloined beach top fluttering gaily from his white whiskered mouth.

Paul and Nikki burst from the door as the cat hit the sidewalk headed for Old Joshua's house. They jumped from the porch and ran after the cat, Nikki falling behind. The high-heeled sandals proved difficult to run in, especially across the rough ground of the backyard.

They chased the cat up the sidewalk to the gate of Old Joshua's place. Paul paused at the gate, looked back for Nikki to catch up. She panted up to Paul's side.

"Where did he go? Did he get away?" she gasped, trying to catch her breath.

"In here," Paul took her hand and lead her through the gate in the high hedge.

"Welcome, children. I'm glad you could make it." Old Joshua stood on the large front porch, the white cat cradled in his arms. "I believe this is yours, Miss," he said, holding out the lavender beach top to Nikki.

She stepped toward the old man, reached out and took the top. "Thanks," she said, not quite knowing how to respond at the moment. She slipped the sheer top over her shoulders.

"I see your face is all better, now that *Mister Dumpty* has taken his spill from the wall."

Nikki's hand went to her face as the smiling old man nodded to her.

"And you young man, you seem to have taken on a few adjustments too," he said, touching his finger to his nose to indicate glasses.

"Little changes here and there," he continued. "But it still remains to be seen what quality an omelette *Mister Dumpty's* remains shall make. Let us hope the cooks do not spoil the dish, what?"

CHAPTER III

Time Out of Phase

"So you know something about the mess we're in," Paul said, calmly addressing the old man. "I've begun to suspect that you have something to do with it."

"I have my part in this," Old Joshua replied.

"As do all of us here." He gestured to indicate the little group in the front yard of the towering Victorian house.

"Yes, I'll bet you had something to do with this morning's disaster," Nikki's voice rang accusingly. "You're probably the spy Apollyon sent to find me and Paul. You probably got to the other three before you found us, didn't you?"

The old man appeared not to have heard Nikki's remark. He addressed Paul directly, "How much have you figured out thus far, young man?"

"Why should I tell you anything?" Paul returned. "I've got a feeling you know a lot more about this than I do, anyway."

"I know what I know," the old man replied. His gaze shifted intently back and forth between Paul and Nikki for a moment, while the cat in his arms gave a deep-throated snarl. "Yes, Gwydion," the old man scratched the cat behind the ears. "I believe you're right. Our friends do seem rather loath to trust us."

"Why do we not go inside?" he asked Nikki and Paul. "There is no merit in our standing in the front yard distrusting one another.

He moved to the door of the large dark house, opened it and beckoned to the two.

"What have we got to lose?" Paul shrugged.

"Come on, let's see what he has to say." Hand in hand, he and Nikki followed the old man and cat into the house.

They entered a large foyer which opened into a huge Victorian living room. Light streamed in through a triptych of immense stained-glass windows, each towering at least ten feet in height. Myriad particles of dust danced in the colored rays of light. The place smelled of fine leathers and old wood, exotic and dry, as if no one had lived there for centuries.

Swords and shields of medieval design were hung on the walls, along with tapestries of rich brocade and large oil portraits of lords in armor and surcoat, and ladies in flowing angel-wing gowns. Next to a great walk-in fireplace stood a gleaming suit of plate armor, with arms resting on a massive two-handed sword, blade point on the ground at its feet.

"Talk about living in a museum," Paul whispered to Nikki as they entered.

"Not really," she said in an undertone, letting go of Paul's hand. "I feel very at home here." Nikki began walking about the room, examining the many curious objects on tables and walls.

"Yes, young lady." The old man took notice of Nikki's curious examination of her surroundings. "Please feel free to look at anything that interests you. I'll put on some tea, then we'll sit down and have a nice long chat."

He put the cat on the floor. "Take good care of our friends, Gwydion," he said as he left the room.

The cat trotted to the middle of the floor where he stopped upon a vast oriental carpet and began licking his fur.

Nikki found herself concentrating deeply on a medieval triptych (a three panel oil painting made of wood, hinged with leather) which sat in the center of the elaborate mantelpiece. Suddenly she became aware of a figure in her peripheral vision.

"Who are you?" she demanded as she spun defensively to meet the stranger.

The cat spat a hiss and jumped to an overstuffed chair. "Who is who?" Paul asked, setting down the figurine he had been examining.

"Didn't you see him?" Nikki gave a bewildered look in Paul's direction. "He was standing right there — at least, I thought I saw someone there."

"Look Nikki, things are spooky enough as is." Paul gave a half-hearted laugh. "Let's not start seeing things that aren't here. We have enough of a problem with the world as it is, or might be, or whatever."

"But I'm sure I saw something! It looked like a tall man with a white moustache, in a long white robe," Nikki insisted. "When I turned around, nobody was there but old whisker-puss." She pointed toward the white cat who now sat purring and licking his fur in the overstuffed chair.

She walked to the chair. The cat stopped his bathing and looked up at her with his round green eyes. A deep guttural meow rolled in his throat.

"I guess it was just my imagination," Nikki finally said. "So much has happened that it's getting hard to tell what's real and what isn't."

"If anything at all is real anymore!" Paul returned. "Remember what Erion said about this only being the way the world might-have-been. One thing for sure is that this world certainly is not the one we began with this morning. Sure, it's a lot like it, but it's not real, at least not what we consider real."

"Speaking of unreal," Nikki said when Paul finished, "come take a look at this triptych." She indicated the work of art on the mantle.

Paul walked to Nikki's side.

"It's some kind of medieval altar piece," Paul noted as he studied the panels. The triptych was composed of three heavy slabs of oak ornately carved around the edges, and hinged together with ancient cracking leather. The scenes of the triptych were painted in oils.

"This thing gives me the creeps," Nikki said.

"Look at those monsters. And what is that thing?" she asked, pointing to the left frame of the triptych.

It depicted what appeared to be a swirling, pulsating octopus. Surrounding the octopus were stars, but the creature looked as if it were absorbing the stars. The upper right of the frame depicted a great black void as if the monster had swept all the stars from that section of space.

The right fame of the triptych portrayed an odd-looking altar scene. A group of figures robed in strange garments were performing weird rites over an altar. Above the altar a black-robed figure was beginning to take form, and inscribed like an arch over the scene were strange words.

"What does that say?" Paul pointed to the wording. "It's hard to read that old script."

"It looks like *Yon-Satheran. Morageth Narletherch Moregeth Yogene-Teth. Yon-Sotharan, Narletheroh-Teth Iga,*" Nikki attempted.

"Meooroew!" The cat leapt from the chair, striking Nikki in the back. The force of the blow caused her to gasp the last word of the inscription. Neither she nor Paul noticed that the words printed on the triptych seemed, for a moment, to glow faintly reddish.

"Darn fool cat!" Nikki shouted as she stumbled into Paul's arms.

"Maybe not," Paul said, as he helped to steady Nikki on her feet again.

"What?"

"Maybe the cat is not a darn fool," he said.

"Take a closer look at the center piece of the triptych."

Nikki looked where Paul pointed. The center piece depicted a great battle between two fantastic creatures. One was a horrible giant who stood on one central leg which grew from the trunk of a grossly deformed body. A single arm projected from the center of its chest. It had only one eye in its hideous face and the deformed head was topped with a wild tuft of unruly hair.

The other creature was a tremendous lionish being. It had great wings which beat the air as it fought and tore at the deformed monster, and fore-legs which looked like those of a giant eagle. Its mane flew about the huge lionish head which seemed to roar with power.

The point where Paul's finger was aimed, though, was behind the lionish creature. There a man stood. He was tall, with a moustache. His white robes flapped in the violence of the battle wind and from his fingertips flew blue fire which struck the one-legged giant on the left arm.

"That's him!" Nikki exploded. "That is the man I saw just a few moments ago, right there." She pointed to the center of the rug. "Right where the cat was sitting."

"'Curiouser and curiouser, said Alice,'" Paul said thoughtfully.

"I see you are admiring my medieval altar piece," the old man's voice broke in. The two turned to see Old Joshua standing in the doorway of the room, a large serving tray in his hands.

"It was done by Jan Van Eyck you know," he added, setting the tray on a table. "It was painted in 1424, shortly after the battle which it depicts."

A look of remembered distress passed across his face.

"That was the last time the Dithreach and I met in battle." He spoke in a far-away voice as he stared at the triptych. "Had Gwydion not struck at that moment I would have been rent asunder. Truly his powers had grown since our prior meeting some centuries earlier when Gwydion struck down a newly rising cult in the south of Wales." The cat gave another of its deep-throated snarls. "That was the last either of us saw of the Dithreach."

"I don't understand," complained Nikki. "I don't see you in the painting and besides, how could you have been alive in the 1400's?"

"After all that has happened this day, do you still doubt such simple matters?" The old man shook his head as if in disbelief.

"And you call the cat Gwydion," Nikki added as if to rebuke something she did not want to let herself believe. "I don't see him in the picture either!"

"Oh, Nikki, do not insist on being such a child. Gwydion is ancient to this world," Old Joshua continued. "He reveals himself as he sees fit, and for now it is as the Cait Sidth. He is most wise among your fellow creatures."

"But..." Nikki began again.

"Do not rebuke me, Nikki!" the old man said, seeming to swell before them, taking on a stern look, as if a tall and powerful being had suddenly filled the old skin Joshua wore.

Nikki stopped before her words could form further. Paul had started to speak, thought better and held his breath.

In a moment Joshua seemed himself again. He motioned to seats about the great fireplace. "Be seated, and I will explain to you exactly what is happening. Then you may inform me of anything you have discovered."

The old man poured tea as if he had all the time in the world, handing the cups to the two as they sat down together on a large divan.

Nikki pulled the beach jacket around her shoulders as she sat, tying it at the neck in front as if that sheer garment would clothe her.

When she accepted the cup of tea from the old man she sat it on a small table beside her; Paul did the same. The old man then crossed the room to the overstuffed chair, took a long stemmed pipe from a stand beside it, and sat down.

"As you no doubt already know," he began as he stuffed the pipe, "creation, as you once knew it, no longer exists."

The cat jumped from the chair he had been sitting in and trotted across the room to Old Joshua, leapt to the arm of the great chair where he stretched out, facing the two.

"I assume you have been contacted by Those-Who-Serve?" he continued.

"We met someone who called himself Erion," Paul replied.

"Ah, Erion is chief of the All-Council." The old man sat forward in the chair, as the cat perked up his ears, and another throaty growl rumbled from him. "We have not heard from Erion since the last great battle," Old Joshua said, his eyes lighting with hope. "What did he have to tell you? Did he give you any instructions?"

"Mer-row!" The cat leapt from the chair arm onto the sofa beside Paul. There he began purring with excitement.

"He didn't tell us anything," Nikki said, dropping her head with the announcement, as if she were letting down a hopeful friend with some unexpected bad news.

The cat spat.

"What?" Joshua came to his feet. "This is madness, child! What can you mean by this? Erion the Ciuthach, All-Wise of the Ferrishyn and High Council of the Firbolgs, summoned you two then had naught to say concerning the death of reality?"

"It wasn't exactly that he didn't say anything," Paul interposed as he stood up before the old man. Nikki sank back against the sofa. "It's just that he didn't say anything more than just what you said. He told us that Apollyon had sort of uncreated everything and that it was up to us and three others who had been saved out of reality to find a way to bring things back."

The cat rumbled its throaty snarl as it moved across the room to curl around Old Joshua's legs.

"Yes, Gwydion," the old man replied to the cat's meow. "It could only be that Erion has failed in his mission and we now stand in a last-ditch effort." Then to Paul and Nikki, Joshua explained, "If what you say is true, then I believe it is beyond our greatest efforts to bring back that which was."

"Then what good can Paul and I hope to do?" Nikki, on the verge of tears, now came to her feet.

"No doubt Erion could not find Gwydion and myself," the old man continued. "He sent you into one aspect of what might-have-been, trusting that we would encounter one another."

"That's what he said," Paul put in. "He said something about acting on those things which may have been in hopes of restoring things."

The old man sat down again, and the cat jumped into his lap. A look of age and fatigue came over Old Joshua's face.

"Sit down," he said gently. "Let us examine the desperate situation in which we find ourselves."

As they sat, Old Joshua began again.

"Paul and Nikki, you know that Erion saved you from destruction at the same moment Apollyon annihilated the rest of reality. But how did he accomplish this?

"Consider that within the course of reality there exist myriad variants on the way things might have happened," Joshua explained. "What would have happened if this or that particular event had not taken place? Everyone has pondered that question many a time.

"Erion selected one of those variants of the way reality might-have-been in which to place you two. Basically we can say that the people, places and things of this world have no substance, no reality. Sadly the people of this world do not even have souls!

"Our quest then is to defeat Apollyon so that this captured "might-have-been" world can become fully real, so that all those destroyed can have a reality in which to regain their very souls!"

"Meoooroew!" the cat rumbled from Joshua's lap.

"Yes, Gwydion," the old man responded. "How indeed. That must be for us to discover."

The cat meowed again.

"Yes, yes. I am well aware of that," Joshua returned. "So much to discover and we still do not know who the fifth member of our party is."

Nikki and Paul looked at one another, then back to the old man and cat.

"I was working on an investigation at the time Apollyon struck," Joshua continued, "and before all was dissolved from reality I was able to freeze a few days in a time loop; to catch them in a phase out of time. Those few days are the only portion of reality left and each time the loop repeats itself it will get smaller until even that ceases to exist. It is to that phase we must travel. I must finish the investigation I have begun. Perhaps that will tell us how it was that Apollyon would have been defeated."

"Merrr, meowrooraw," the cat growled.

"Indeed, Gwydion," the old man returned.

"That will be of no value to us now but perhaps it will lead us to find who the fifth member of our little band is to be. Without the entire fellowship we have no hope at all."

"How do we get to this, this, phase out of time you set up?" Paul asked.

The old man rose as he spoke. "We shall fly on the time winds," he replied. The cat returned another of his growls. "And that, my dear friends, is in itself a dangerous and tricky business even under the best of circumstances, and we have the minions of Apollyon looking for us to add to the matter.

"Come." He turned, waving at them to follow. "You shall now see me as I truly am."

He lead them through the huge old house. They passed through many strange and interesting rooms until they finally came to a back door. Joshua placed the cat on the floor, opened the door and lead the way into the backyard.

It was getting late in the afternoon and the sun cast a great shadow across the yard from the giant sycamore tree behind Nikki's house.

She saw a brief movement at the kitchen door of her house which looked like Harold going inside.

"Come," the old man beckoned again. Nikki, Paul and the cat followed Old Joshua across the yard, through a gate in the hedge wall at the back, and into the vacant lot behind Nikki's house. They came to a halt beneath the spreading bows of the giant sycamore tree. The old man raised his arms as he turned to face Paul and Nikki.

"Behold," he said, his voice rolling like thunder. "Joshua is but one of many names by which I am called. Look you now upon the form of the one whom friends have come to call Counselor!"

The air around Old Joshua began to shimmer, and the old man himself began to glow and change form. He radiated, pulsed and grew until finally there stood before them the great lion-like creature of the altar piece in the old house.

The maned head rolled back in a mighty roar. Great eagle wings beat in mighty rhythm and powerful taloned forefeet clawed the air as the creature reared on its hind legs.

As the beast came down onto all fours it turned its magnificent head to Nikki and Paul. While it spoke, the white cat leapt upon Counselor's back. "Climb upon my back, my children." His voice shook the air. "The time we seek grows ever shorter as we tarry."

Nikki felt as if her legs had just turned to milk toast. She turned to face Paul.

"I guess it's not so strange when you consider all that's happened so far today," he said. "Shall we hop aboard?"

"Uh..." Nikki nodded a slight affirmative.

"Uh huh." Her voice seemed to be elsewhere at the moment.

Paul picked her up and placed her astride Counselor's massive back. He hopped up in front of her.

"Well and good," Counselor roared. "I told you once before, Nikki my child, gryphons never lie, and I promise that I will do my best to take care on our journey."

The mighty wings beat the air as the beast rose from the ground. The giant sycamore fell beneath them and the world shimmered away and they passed into a misty blueness as a strong wind whipped up about them.

CHAPTER IV

Altered Phases

*C*ounselor's great wings beat a heavy rhythm as he bore his charges upward. Slowly the time winds built in intensity. What had begun as a strong blue wind soon became a driving gale roaring in Nikki's ears. Counselor's wings stopped their beating and spread to catch the force of the howling blueness. He banked sharply right and began to climb on the force of the incoming gale.

The time storm lashed about Nikki and Paul, stinging them slightly as if it carried unseen grains of sand that left their skin burning.

"The time winds blow strongly," Counselor roared above the howl of the gale. "Surely the enemy seeks us." He dropped sharply and leveled, without Nikki, Paul or the Cait Sidth slipping even slightly across his back.

His great wings beat several powerful strokes as he sought his bearing in the storming time winds. He paused for a moment in mid-flight, then arched his great body, side-slipping them into a powerful updraft like that of an elevator ride, making Nikki's stomach plunge.

Counselor leaned hard into the updraft, causing him to spiral upward in tight dizzying circles. Nikki and Paul bent forward, holding to the gryphon's body for dear life.

As the swirling circles became tighter and faster, Nikki wanted to scream, but something held her back. Beneath her she could feel the muscles in Counselor's back as they contracted and relaxed, shifted and pulled while the gryphon strove to battle the raging time winds and to ensure a secure seat for his charges. That alone kept Nikki's scream back, for even through the raging time winds she could

feel a reassuring power coursing through Counselor's body.

Nikki shut her eyes against the sickening vertigo as the spirals grew tighter and faster. Then, without warning, they shot from the maelstrom like a pea from a shooter.

The gryphon lashed fiercely with his wings to balance himself and his charges as they broke from the temporal vortex. Counselor bucked like a bronco as he attempted to bring his wild flight under control without losing his riders. The vision of his companions falling helplessly from his back and into the bellowing eternity of the storm below gave fire to his struggle.

Reaching their apex, they slowed and Counselor resumed his steady forward pull. Below they could see the raging time gale as the gryphon flew the calm breezes in wordless exhaustion.

Paul started to speak but a clawed paw from Gwydion dug itself into his leg. "*He will need all his mind to find the pathway back in,*" a thought pressed itself on Paul's mind as the claws caught his leg. "*Do not break his concentration.*"

Paul looked down at the cat on his lap. It stared back with glassy eyes. He thought twice about speaking, reached down and stroked the cat's back. The claws eased from his leg and Paul felt a rumble within the cat as it snarled its approval of his decision.

The companions leaned forward against Counselor as the gryphon veered hard, following the calmer elements above the storm. He selected particular currents of the time winds as a skilled woodsman picks familiar trails through a forest. For what seemed like hours, the company glided on the time currents as the gryphon expertly piloted their way. Then something caught Nikki's eye.

"What's that?" she shouted, over the rush of the time winds.

"Good girl, Nikki," Counselor roared. "You have seen it even before I. That is the gate I have been looking for!"

The gryphon flew toward a sight Paul was only now picking out. It appeared as a shimmer of pale blue in the time mist, reminding Paul of heat shimmers on a hot summer day.

The gryphon's great wings beat several hard strokes against the time winds and the company shot like an arrow toward its goal.

"Hold tight, children," Counselor's voice boomed, his great muscled frame straining against the winds. "This is going to be a tricky entry, for the dimension gate is nearly closed. If we miss, we will be stranded within the vortex for eternity!"

The shimmer swept closer and closer. It had a decidedly disorienting effect, and Nikki felt as if she could not hold on. She surely would have fallen if not for the skill of Counselor in keeping the riders on his back.

Suddenly the gryphon gave a mighty forward beat with his wings. He reared up like a roped stallion, his front legs beating the air, he threw his great maned head back and let sound a mighty roar which seemed to shake the very foundations of eternity.

As he roared, the shimmer seemed to part like a curtain revealing blue sky and clouds beyond. With a mighty pump of his wings, Counselor shot through.

Blue sky, white clouds and the fresh smell of summer air reached them as they passed through the shimmer and away from the time winds. The gryphon circled as he began his descent. Nikki and Paul recognized South Shores below them — they sailed over familiar houses and to the very backyard from which they had left. Counselor landed with a strong flapping of his wings right beside the same sycamore tree from which they had begun their journey.

"Merrroow!" The Cait Sidth leapt to the ground.

"I can't say that I would want to do that every day!" Paul exclaimed as he climbed from the gryphon's back. "I feel like I should fall down and kiss the ground!" He turned to help Nikki down.

After the girl climbed from his back, the gryphon stretched and reared. He shimmered and glowed, and began to shrink. In a moment only Old Joshua stood where the mighty form of Counselor had been.

"Yes, Paul, it was a difficult journey, but I fear the toughest part lies yet ahead of us," Old Joshua said.

"Meerowf," groused the Cait Sidth.

"You are right, Gwydion. I suppose that "tough" is an understatement, since we have all of Creation to save, of which Man's portion has already been destroyed.

"My head is still swimming from all of this," said Nikki. "Your cat is an ancient wizard, you are a gryphon, we just flew through heaven only knows what, and an archdemon is out to kill us. I'm still not sure I even believe all this, but I'm beginning to get a grip on the idea."

"Meeerrroooorrowww!" the Cait Sidth rubbed around her legs.

"I think so too, Gwydion," Joshua said, looking down at the white furry form. "Our Nikki is beginning to catch on. Come on you three, I have some work set up for us inside."

Nikki took one step and the world swirled in a haze about her. The music of the mad pipers had begun again, and her scream trailed from her own hearing as she slipped into unconsciousness.

* * *

Nikki awoke to a throbbing disco beat pounding into her head, and a cold floor against her right cheek. As she opened her eyes, she was almost blinded by flashes of blue, followed by red, then yellow. Her mind was grasping for something tangible as she passed out again.

"I told you not to let her snort those poppers, Rae," a slender man in a white jacket chastised his neighbor at a long, mirror-lined bar.

"Butt out, Danny!" Rae pushed off from the bar and headed for the dance floor. "I can take care of her."

Rae stalked across the dance floor, its inlaid panels flashing alternating colors beneath her feet as disco lights whirled overhead. She reached Nikki and stooped to lift the semiconscious girl into a sitting position.

A horrible reality screamed into Nikki's awakening, as hands from a hundred miles away manipulated her body. She tried opening her eyes again. "Hey, hon," Rae said, her eyes meeting Nikki's. Nikki struggled to clear her vision, taking in the strange young woman who was holding her in her arms. "Welcome back to the real world."

"Rae?" Nikki slurred. Where had that name come from and who was this person in a red-flannel shirt talking to her? Where in creation was she?

Danny picked out the red of Rae's shirt through the crowd of dancers; saw Rae attempting unsuccessfully to bring Nikki to her feet. The disco lights suddenly switched to a rapidly flashing white strobe lending an unearthly staccato effect to the self-absorbed dancers. Almost against his better judgement, Danny started toward the two girls.

"Need some help?" Danny crouched next to Rae, who had managed to get half of Nikki sitting upright, like a rag doll on the dance floor. Rae snapped a menacing look at Danny.

"I told you to butt out! We're through, you and me, okay? I can handle her!"

"Sure thing Ms. Independent!" Danny sneered. He watched the two of them for a moment. Nikki was wearing a pair of white lace stockings, garter belt, white high-heeled sandals and a black frock coat buttoned with only three buttons. Danny reached out a hand and pulled the corner of Nikki's coat-dress over a section of very bare hip and thigh.

"Well, my dear, you might be able to handle her, but let's not give any of her secrets away while you try your hand at it."

Rae grabbed Danny by the lapel, and cocked her fist back to deliver.

"I told you to get out of my face, jerk!" Time seemed to freeze for a moment as the two squatted, poised in the midst of dancing revelers who either couldn't care less about what was going on or were as blind to someone else's problems as are most people.

Rae lost her grip on his jacket as Danny rose to his feet.

"I just care about the kid, that's all," Danny said, brushing his lapel. He looked down at Nikki, struggling to open her eyes. "If you need me later, Rae, don't look me up!" He turned and strode back to the bar.

Nikki's eyes focused.

"Come on, Nick, I've got to get you up and out of here," Rae encouraged. She rose to her feet, pulling Nikki upright with her. Nikki's eyes locked onto Rae's and flashed.

"Get away from me!" Nikki pushed Rae with all her might. The facts of this might-have-been reality had just crashed into Nikki's brain like a ton of hot lead. The two stared at each other for a moment, Nikki's eyes flashing violet fire. She met the cold stare of Rae's black eyes in cosmic combat. Long moments passed as Nikki saw the starkness of her own reality building within Rae's ebony gaze. The music of the dance club faded into the distance as the two stood, locked into each other's gaze.

"*Let her in,*" began a voice far back in Nikki's mind. "*This could be real if you just let her in,*" the voice grew stronger.

"*So what if it is not what you want, think about everyone else! Reality must be saved.*" The slightest hint of mad piping sounded, then faded into a recess of her mind.

"Take me home, Rae, can we go now?" Nikki took Rae's hand, accepting the other girl's help to stay on her feet.

"Sure, hon," Rae replied, pulling Nikki closer, supporting her weight. "You've had a tough night, kid. We'll get you right into bed."

They made their way from the dance floor to the bar where Rae paid up her bill and retrieved her

jacket. They left the backway with Rae still supporting most of Nikki's weight. The girl seemed to be
walking on limp spaghetti. Rae poured Nikki into
the car.

"Don't worry, kid," she said, brushing hair
from Nikki's eyes as she leaned across her. "We'll
be home soon and we'll get you settled in for the
night. Everything is going to be all right."

"Don't drive too fast, okay?" Nikki's voice
sounded like that of a little lost girl.

"Sure, kid, don't worry." Rae gave her a pat on
the head and closed Nikki's car door.

The young woman walked around her '65
Pontiac thoughtfully, and slid in behind the steer-
ing wheel. She started the engine and drove from
the club parking lot, winding through city streets in
silence, but within Rae's head the sounds of all the
past times which had gone so much like this night
threatened to deafen her.

Never in their year and a half of living together
had Rae seen Nikki so burned out. Nikki had always been nervous and Rae had figured the kid was
holding her wits together by nothing more than
their being together. She knew Nikki depended
entirely on her — not that Rae needed anyone, but
Nikki was a classic case of one neurotic jump-off to
the next. In spite of her youth, Nikki had been

through so many relationships that Rae had lost count. The woman had tried to figure what was driving the girl to such lengths but to no avail. Even just a meaningless jilt from someone picked up a week earlier in a bar could be enough to send Nikki back to the pill bottle. Rae knew Nikki could not go through that again. Nikki needed Rae's support bad, but she needed professional help, too. Rae was at her wit's end as to what to do about this.

By the time they reached the house, Nikki was sound asleep. Rae went to the porch and unlocked the door, then returned to the car to get Nikki. Rae carried the sleeping girl to her bed, took her clothes off and pulled the covers over her.

Rae bent to kiss the girl on the cheek, then went into the living room where she read *Virginia Woolf* until she fell asleep in the chair. At four a.m. she awoke to the sound of a dog barking down the block. She got up, stripped off her bar costume as she walked to the bedroom, then crawled into bed.

✳ ✳ ✳

"Where's Nikki?" Paul shouted.

"What?" Joshua spun around.

"RRRReeeerrrrrooooooooooorrrrrrrrr!!" Gwydion rumbled, then bowed and spat.

"She was standing here a moment ago, and then poof!" Paul threw his hands up in exclamation.

"She has been grabbed by the minions of Apollyon!" Joshua said, his voice heavy.

The Cait Sidth growled, walking around and around the spot where Nikki had stood only moments before.

"Yes, my friend," Old Joshua answered the Cait Sidth. "This means I may not get the research finished we came here for."

"But won't that..." Paul began.

"It doesn't matter what it will do," Old Joshua interrupted quickly. "Nikki is in grave danger. If I can't find her and get her back, not only will she be lost forever in the mind of Apollyon, but our entire mission will surely fail. Let us go inside."

The three turned toward the house. Gwydion bounded up the back porch steps and dashed in through a swinging pet door. Paul walked beside Old Joshua.

"Hey Pauley," called a voice from the next yard. Paul and Joshua looked across the hedge into Nikki's yard. Harold was standing on the back porch waving.

"Hey, Harold," Paul responded, waving.

"Have you seen my sister?" the boy called.

"As a matter of fact, I was just going to look for her," Paul returned, not sure whether he should take the reality of Harold seriously or not.

"Wait a minute!" Harold shouted, then jumped from the porch, disappearing behind the hedge fencing in Old Joshua's yard. A moment later the brush rattled and Harold crawled out through a small gap in the hedge. The way it had been trimmed, a branch thick with leaves had hidden the passage through the hedge which was just large enough to let a person crawl through.

"My dad says you're a harmless old kook," the teen boldly announced to Old Joshua as he strode up.

"Well, your dad may be absolutely right," Old Joshua returned. "Anyway, why don't you come inside with us? We were just going to have some ginger cakes and hot tea, then maybe you can help us find your sister."

"Do you think he is..?" Paul began.

Joshua interrupted Paul's question. "I certainly do."

"I hope you like surprises," Paul said, looking expectantly at Harold.

"Are you sure that old guy is safe, Paul?" Harold squinted up at the two.

"Kid, you don't know the half of it." Paul clapped a hand onto his buddy's shoulder. "Come on inside and prepare to have your brain fried!"

"Wait a second. I'll be right back!" The boy dashed from Paul, darted through the hedge, and then in a moment's time was back through. He carried a skateboard with a large purple dragon painted on it and the word "Executioner" blazoned across it.

"I never go anywhere without my wheels, man," he grinned.

"Now what about those goodies you promised?"

"Come inside, Paul and Harold, time is of the essence," Joshua said, escorting the boys up the steps and through the back door into the kitchen of his huge house.

There was tea on the stove and freshly made ginger cakes on the table.

"Paul, will you bring the refreshments for Harold in the living room? I must go upstairs for a few moments. Try to explain some of what is happening to our friend while I am busy."

"Sure thing," Paul returned. The old man nodded, opened a door and slipped up a stairway.

"Man, are you going to flip over this," Paul said, grinning at Harold in a way that made Harold think for a moment that his sister's boyfriend may well be the most dangerous person in the whole neighborhood.

Joshua entered the room at the top of the stairs. The room smelled of old books and was lit, like the living room below, by the light of a stained glass window. The Cait Sidth was curled up on a gigantic book which looked several hundred years old. It was lettered by hand and the open pages were illuminated by beautiful medieval artwork.

"I see you have already begun work," Joshua said, as he entered the room. The Cait Sidth snarled his reply.

"I didn't think so," Joshua replied. "Seems like you always leave the hard part for me." He moved to a table in the center of the room where he lifted a purple and gold silk cloth to reveal a crystal ball.

The Cait Sidth snarled.

"I don't care what you did five hundred years ago," the old man replied as he set the cloth aside. Again the Cait Sidth snarled.

"Do not argue with me, Gwydion, we have been together too many years for you to slip a fancy-turned word past me. Now just be so kind as to read out the proper incantation."

Gwydion snarled again, got up and walked around in a circle three times on the book.

"Will you stop wasting time, we must find that young girl and bring her back!"

"Rrruferg!" the Cait Sidth snarled back before getting up again and walking to the top of the book. There he stood for a moment, looking intently at the page. Then he opened his mouth and, in a very human-sounding voice, began reading out some long-forgotten language understood only by himself and Joshua.

The crystal ball began to glow as Joshua watched.

✳ ✳ ✳

Paul was getting a very condescending look from Harold, who had just laid his hand on Paul's shoulder.

"You are totally and completely crazy," Harold said, speaking slowly and distinctly into Paul's face. "Either my sister is in love with a complete nut, or you take me for the dumbest jerk in the world. Get real, Paul, we live in the space age! Guys don't fall for this kind of stuff, anymore. We're into computers now, not fairy tales."

"Mmerrrrooooooooww!" Gwydion bounded down the stairs.

"Raaammp!" In two leaps he went from the top landing of the stairs to the bottom, then into Paul's lap.

"Ouch! Watch the claws!" Paul half rose, grabbing at the Cait Sidth as it pounced onto him.

"Reow!" the cat snarled, looking directly into Paul's eyes. It then bowed and hissed, leapt from the boy's lap and pranced anxiously about.

"What is it, Lassie? Do you want us to follow you?" Harold asked, mocking the cat.

"Don't make fun of him, Harold," Paul advised. "He does want us to follow him, come on!"

"Give me a break!" Harold smirked, reluctantly rising to follow Paul and the Cait Sidth.

Gwydion lead the young men up the stairs and down a long hall. Doors lined the hall and at the far end another stairway lead to a third story. Up this stairway the Cait Sidth lead them to a single door at the top.

"Merrrrow!" he yowled as he approached the door. It swung open, seemingly on its own power. The cat bounded through with the guys on his heels.

"Good, you've brought them," Joshua said. He turned from the crystal ball on the table, and spoke to the cat as the three entered the room. "We've found her."

"What, found Nikki?" Paul blurted out. "Oh, fantastic! Is she okay? Where is she? How do we get her back?"

"Jehosaphat! What is all this? You some kind of gypsy or something?" Harold scratched his head and gawked about the wizard's room in amazement.

"Over here, Paul." Old Joshua motioned Paul toward himself and the crystal ball. "She is in another might-have-been, as I suspected — one of Apollyon's design."

"What are you talking about?" Harold walked over to the table and stared into the ball. It pulsed, swirling with lights and mist.

"Please be quiet for a moment, Harold, while I talk with Paul. I will try to answer your questions shortly." The old man then addressed Paul. "She had been snatched from us in an attempt to break our fellowship and keep us from succeeding in bringing back a reality. My guess is that since Nikki is our weakest link, so to speak, he struck at her."

"Where is she, Joshua?" Paul asked. "If she is not in the vortex, where did Apollyon take her and when are we going to go after her?"

"I am afraid that we cannot go after her, Paul."

"What? What are you saying? I thought you and Gwydion were such great wizards and everything. We just can't leave her off in some nether world in Apollyon's clutches!"

"Rrreeeeooow!"

"Easy, Paul," Joshua soothed. "I said nothing about leaving her. I only said we could not go and get her. What I was going to say, if you had let me finish, was that we have to send someone to get her."

"Alright! Hey, that's okay, as long as we get her back. Let's get her back right now!"

Harold had wandered to a bookshelf and was helping himself to some reading material.

"Merow!" Gwydion leapt to a table next to him

"Nice kitty," Harold said, reaching out to pet the Cait Sidth. Gwydion immediately stung his hand away with a lightening slap of a white paw.

"Put my book back where you got it from, boy!" The cat spoke perfectly to Harold.

"What? I... but, I..."

"I tried to tell you but no, you're into computers and don't believe this kind of stuff," Paul said. He had witnessed the entire event while Joshua had been talking. The old man now turned to the younger boy.

"Please do what Gwydion has asked you," he said. "Those are ancient and valuable tomes. You may hurt one of them, or even yourself if you tried to read anything."

"But... but... but..."

"Harold, I've already told you everything that has happened since this morning, so just get used to it, okay?"

"Paul is right, Harold," Joshua added, walking to the younger boy and looking him right in the eye. "You can either help or not. You are the fifth member of our fellowship, like it or not. If you choose not to help, then all that is, or was, becomes of no more account than the oblivion of Apollyon's mind."

Harold stood as if stunned, and looked from Paul, to Joshua, to Gwydion, to the book in his hand. Slowly he replaced the book on the shelf.

"What can I do to help?" He faced Joshua squarely, and his young face was set with a fresh-born determination.

"Paul is going to help Gwydion and myself here with our magic and research while we send you into a strange realm of existence where you will rescue your sister from a life that might-have-been hers if she had run away from home when she was thirteen-years-old. You will then try to find a way to get her back together with us. Paul, Gwydion and I will be working from this end to send power and knowledge to you, but much of the work will be up to you."

"When do we start?" Harold asked. "Get your skateboard from downstairs first," Joshua said, smiling. "I don't think you should be sent anywhere without, as you say, your wheels."

CHAPTER V

Ordeal in Otherwhere

*T*he night brought back the dreams which had been gaining in intensity over the past few weeks. In a disembodied state, Nikki saw a world of surrealistic terror stretching before her. Great black monoliths towered miles in height, dark ooze dripping from them as fiery runes of unknown tongues steamed upon their titanic faces.

Then she was in her body and walking amongst those towering monoliths, the stark terror of their size and the hissing runes of cold fire pressing a horror upon the girl known only in the most lucid nightmares.

Then there were the footsteps. These were felt more than heard, as if some gigantic figure were lumbering beneath the earth itself. Great slogging footsteps thudded like the skin drums of some long forgotten priesthood. And the fear which preceded this creature carried the edge of stark insanity, cutting the heart from Nikki as the titan neared the place where she stood. Though miles beneath her, the mind of the lumbering titan probed like a fiery poker, searching for her. She could not run, she could not scream. All she could do was endure the oppression of those monoliths, whose terror came from the surrealism of being totally out of proportion to any sane measurement.

There were also voices. They sounded like voices of men, chanting in some long-forgotten tongue and in perfect rhythm to the footfalls which rose from within the bowels of the earth.

Finally, Nikki was able to run. She ran and she screamed and the earth quaked about her. Towering monoliths began to crumble as the earth rippled; they began to break up and start a slow-motion descent from their towering heights. As Nikki ran, the earth ripped like rotten cloth. From its depths rose a gargantuan, a many-tentacled head wreathed in sulphurous fumes. Tentacles lashed toward the running girl as jets and geysers of brimstone and sulphur-laden steam roared into the air, a fiery dance adding its madness to the symphony of terror.

"Now I've got you," the monstrosity mind-blasted its words into her head. "I have you, Nikki Renn, my old enemy, and now as I promised long ago, you will finally belong to me!"

* * *

Morning light hazed through the bedroom windows and with it came the angry sound of blackbirds bickering in a tree outside. It was a huge elm which was dying of blight, and from its blighted branches the angry birds rasped their hostilities. Nikki woke from her nightmare feeling like a demon was pounding the inside of her skull with a fire axe.

"Oh God, my head!" She moaned as she sat up.

Nikki managed to drag herself out of bed. The night terrors had drained all her normal morning energy. With her feet feeling like wet sandbags, she sludged to the bathroom. Robot-like, she went through her morning ritual.

It was not until after Nikki had brushed her teeth and started with her hair that she "almost-remembered" something; she had a vague feeling akin to the feeling people get when they are at the check-out in a grocery store thinking there was something they were supposed to get but were unable to remember what it might be.

She tried to pin down the ethereal almost-memory as she brushed her hair, but it continued to evade her. Finally, after a hundred strokes, she put down her brush and walked to the kitchen where she started making breakfast. At least, she thought to herself, the headache had gone away.

It was the smell of frying bacon that first entered Rae's sleeping state and told her there was another world besides the one of dreams which was now commanding her undivided attention. She rolled over too close to the edge, and nearly fell out of bed. That was the jolt which drove sleep back into the realm where it hides during the day.

Rae sat up and stretched. "Smells like breakfast to me!" Rae shouted through the house.

"If you can make it in here you might get to eat some of it," Nikki called back.

Rae went from bed to bathroom to kitchen in record time.

"Nice breakfast, kid." She came up behind Nikki, eying the pan of fresh eggs over her shoulder. "What was all that with Danny at the Power Supply last night?" Nikki queried, scooping eggs onto the plates.

"That jerk," Rae said, placing the filled plates on the table. "He gets his kicks out of sticking his nose in my business. It's like a hobby with him, so I told him to buzz off. We're not going back to the Power Supply, since that's where he hangs out."

"But I like it," Nikki protested, sitting down to her breakfast. She started to take a bite of eggs but ended up staring blankly at the fork, which she had stopped halfway to her mouth.

"Darn it, Nikki." Rae picked up her fork. "We can go dancing at Electra from now on."

"But they don't have the sound system Power Supply has, and besides, it's cheap and dirty there!" Eggs danced across the table as she threw down her fork.

"I am not going to hang out at any place that Danny haunts!"

"He's a nice guy and he really likes us! I don't see why you get so ripped at him. What has he ever done to hurt you anyway?"

"I just don't like him anymore, okay?" Rae fired a hostile look at Nikki, who sat in silence as Rae took a bite of eggs. "You'd better eat before your food gets cold."

"But why can't we go to the Power Supply, Rae? I want to!"

"Damn it, Nikki, there's nothing more depressing than a know-it-all like Danny who makes his life's work out of getting into everybody's business. I can't stand him, period! That's all, end of comment."

"I know there's more to it than that." Nikki took her first bite of the eggs.

"Okay, okay, OKAY! I can't stand him because the jerk has nothing better to do than waste my time lecturing me on how I'm corrupting your morals or something. He's constantly ragging me that because you're too young to decide what you want in life. He told me I ought to pack you up and send you back to your mommy and daddy."

"Rae, you know I'm here because I want to be." Nikki put her fork down and looked the other girl squarely in the face. "I'm old enough to know what I'm doing and to make my own choices. I choose how I live my life."

"Yeah hon, I'm glad." Rae dropped her gaze from Nikki to hide the look of distress which filled her face.

"So ignore Danny and let's live our own lives, okay?"

"Yeah, Nick," Rae answered, with her newly-found smile, okay."

* * *

Old Joshua handed Harold a brown parchment scroll. "Here, Harold, unroll this and read it. Study it carefully."

Harold took the ancient, crackling manuscript and puzzled over it for a moment.

"Are you kidding? This looks like chicken tracks!" Harold protested.

Joshua, his eyes closed in concentration, held his right hand above the boy's head for a moment.

"*Elio Obley-Ania Vory-Nahlia Montigly-Anoay,*" the old man muttered. He encouraged Harold, "Once again, my lad. I believe you can read it if you really try."

When the boy shrugged and looked again, a realization crept over him that although he had never before seen the letters in front of him, he now not only knew how to pronounce the words, but he could also understand their meanings.

A strange heat rushed from his fingertips through his body as he read the scroll. "My fingertips feel funny," Harold said slowly, looking at his hands. Then his intuition broke through. "I feel power," he said. "It just felt like fire ran from my hands right up my arms!"

"So it is, my boy. That which you feel in your hands is power, and you shall know how to use it when the time is right." Joshua continued, "And what you felt was your first dose of what most people call magic."

"What are you saying?" Harold looked up from the scroll.

"What are you talking about?"

"Reow!" Gwydion jumped onto the table in front of Harold.

"Just as you say, Gwydion. We have recognized the special potential of our young friend." Joshua then addressed Harold again. "As Gwydion and I were doing our research to find Nikki we made a discovery — we saw you helping in our mission and wielding power such as Gwydion wields. Harold, you and Gwydion are of the same blood."

Harold carefully laid down the scroll before the Cait Sidth, looked at it for a minute, then turned his eyes to Joshua.

"What exactly does all this mean?" His voice, although calm, brimmed with uncertainty.

"I mean that you are a wizard by birth, my boy," Joshua answered. "I mean that you are rare among humans, rare because you were born with the ability to understand and manipulate the physics of the multi universe in a way that others call magic."

"You're kidding, right?" Harold asked hopefully.

"Absolutely not."

"And I can..." He darted his hands forward, mimicking a magician, "cast a spell?"

"You will be learning to," the old man smiled at him, "and Gwydion will be your teacher. But first we must save your sister or we will have no world in which you can learn your art. Do you get my drift?"

"I'm afraid I do," the boy answered. "And as Paul told me when he introduced me to this weird adventure, the world where Nikki has been taken is a part of Apollyon's imagination. If we do not convince her of that and get her out of there, everything in the universe is doomed. Seems simple enough. Any kid could understand it!"

"Humor is useful in arduous situations," the old man observed wryly. "Now my boy, are you ready to go?"

Harold picked up his skateboard and nodded a determined smile in Paul's direction.

"I'm ready, Josh."

Aided by Gwydion, the old man began an incantation. Harold saw Joshua, Gwydion, and Paul begin to shimmer, then sleepiness hit the lad and the last thing he heard was the voice of Paul calling good luck.

The drowsy feeling passed in a moment when he realized that he was standing in a grassy park. "Wow, what a way to travel!" said Harold as he staggered a couple of steps after full materialization. The boy dropped the skateboard on a wide sidewalk and pushed off.

"I guess the first thing to do is find out exactly where I am," he said aloud.

He zigged and zagged about the park looking for any landmark familiar to him. Ten minutes later he came to a large sign advertising the park to the public.

"At least I know I'm in Chicago's Lincoln Park. The zoo's here! Hey, that's where I'll look for Nikki... the Monkey House!"

"Hey, kid." A big blue cop seemed to spring out of nowhere.

"Are you lost?"

"No, officer. Actually I'm a wizard from another dimension and I'm here looking for my sister who should be around here somewhere."

"Well, Mister Wizard, just as long as you're not out here alone when I come back through." The officer smiled, nodded, and kept on his way.

"Great, and now I have the cops to look out for! I don't suppose running about in the grass and shouting 'Hey, Nikki' would help. I sure wish Joshua and Puss 'n Boots had given me some kind of 'Nikki compass' or something. Good gosh, Nikki, where would you be in this toddling town?"

Harold kicked his board up into his hands and trudged along the sidewalk, winding his way through Lincoln Park.

"Hey, what do I have to worry about, I'm a wizard!" he said optimistically. "But I sure am hungry!" he added, walking over to a vendor's peanut cart. He dug into his pocket for fifty cents which he plopped down on the vendor's cart.

Munching the peanuts, he dropped his board, mounted, pushed off and gained speed as he rounded a slight curve ahead of him. "What do wizards do in situations like this?" he asked himself, chewing on the freshly cooked nuts. "Where is Gwydion when I need to ask?"

He cupped his hands to his mouth. "Here kitty, kitty, kitty!" he called through a mouthful. In a moment he brought the board to a halt. "Maybe if I just clapped my hands..."

Harold sat the bag of peanuts on his skateboard and then clapped his hands three times.

"What in the world..." A burning rush tingled through his hands. It felt as if fire were coursing through his veins and slowly moving up into his arms.

"Whoa, here. I completely forgot about the spell I read. I guess dimension travel scrambles the brain. Old Josh said I would know when and how to use it!"

He stepped from his skateboard and stared at his burning hands stretched before him. He turned them over and back, staring at them.

"Let's see what we have here." He began turning in tight circles. "Bingo!" he shouted. "The burning definitely increases or decreases according to the direction I'm facing.

"So you did give me a Nikki compass. Well, this is great! Hey, what do you think you're doing?" he asked, turning back to his skateboard where a fat gray park squirrel sat eating the last peanuts from the bag. "Oh heck, help yourself." He plopped cross-legged into the grass. The squirrel took momentary note of the boy's actions, then resumed eating.

"You know anything about wizards, fuzzy?" Harold asked the furry rodent. "I mean, you wouldn't happen to be one in disguise would you? I know one who is a cat." The squirrel looked at Harold, tossed an empty peanut shell to the ground and grabbed the last one from the bag. "No, I guess you wouldn't be, would you?" he said to the squirrel who was more interested in sniffing the now empty bag than listening to Harold.

As he stood up, the squirrel dashed into a tree and back up into the canopy of limbs overhead. Harold took a directional reading, mounted his board and took off in the direction which caused the most intense heat to radiate from his hands.

The skateboarder coasted along a sidewalk which wound its way out of Lincoln Park. Harold soon found himself surfing the sidewalk of Lakeshore drive without the slightest idea of where he was going, save for the slight feeling of heat which rose and fell in the palms of his hands, according to the direction he turned.

For twenty minutes he continued his winding trip through the windy city, following the "Nikki compass" of his hands, then he drew up short. A sudden felling of foreboding swept over him like an icy wave. Something was the matter with Nikki.

"*Concentrate on your art for power, Harold!*" the voice seemed to pulse from deep within his skull and Harold knew it was the voice of Gwydion.

"What power?" He kicked his skateboard up into his hands and turned round and around looking up into the tops of the buildings facing him as if he expected to see the face of the big white cat looking down at him.

"*Reooooowwww!*" The sound of a great cat snarled from deep within his head. "*Concentrate, Harold, you MUST know the words!*"

"Great!" He dropped his skateboard, clapping the top of it with his foot as it hit the pavement. "The *Cat-in-the-Hat* wants me to play guessing games."

For a moment he was too agitated to do more than stand in his tracks and fume.

"Nikki, where are you?"

"*Concentrate,*" the voice called distantly within his brain.

He kicked the skateboard to the edge of the sidewalk and sat down on it. Cupping his chin in his hands he began to concentrate on Nikki. He tried to picture her in his mind, and in a moment the memory of her standing at the head of the stairs that morning came to him. He saw her in his mind's eye, a look of distress on her face from nearly having fallen down the stairs because of his skateboard. Then he remembered his laughing tease, as if he really had not cared if she had fallen and gotten hurt.

It was then he realized how much he did love his sister. He had lashed out at her with his taunts because her nearly getting hurt had been due to his neglect, and that had embarrassed him.

"I'm sorry I hurt you, Nikki," Harold spoke aloud. "If I ever get you back I won't be so self-centered, I'll pay attention to your needs, always..."

His thought was broken by a sudden burst of fear that shot through him and caused him to sit bolt upright.

"No! I won't let it become real!" Nikki's voice rolled from the air around him and a deathly fear sunk into his heart, a fear he instantly knew Nikki was feeling at that moment wherever she was. He sprung to his feet.

It was then the words came to him.

"*El Elyon Eloi Shaddi Shaddoniah, Adonoi Lama Shabathenoli, El-Kahnahania!*"

He shouted the words as if he had known them all his life, as if they were no more than a child's rhyme learned on his mother's knee. As they left his mouth the eastern sky flashed lightening and a peal of thunder crackled like the word of God over the city.

The fire in his hands began to burn hotter.

"Was that me or whisker-puss?" he muttered to himself as he watched the flickering sky. "Or has Apollyon finally pinned Nikki down? I'd better get a move on it!"

He circled, taking a reading from his hands, kicked his board back to the sidewalk and shoved off.

* * *

"Okay, so maybe I can keep my temper under control with Danny," Rae said as she washed the breakfast dishes.

Nikki sat on the clothes washer swinging her legs.

"Okay, we'll keep going to the Power Supply. It's worth it to see you happy, Nikki."

Nikki stared out the door which led from the kitchen into the backyard. She could not stop feeling that there was something very important she was forgetting.

"So it's all a matter of what we think, right, kid?"

"Huh?" Nikki suddenly realized that Rae had been talking about something and she had not heard a word of it.

"Hey, what are you lost in space about?" Rae turned and dried her hands on a towel by the sink. "I don't think you've heard a thing I've said for the last ten minutes."

"I don't know what, but something is bothering me today and I just can't get my head straight."

"Don't worry, hon." Rae draped the towel over the dish drainer.

Nikki hopped down from her seat on the washer and walked to Rae.

"Listen." Rae reached out and put her arms around Nikki's neck, a strange blackness swirling in the woman's eyes. "It's just you and me from now on. I'll protect you from all your troubles here. From now on it's going to be our own little world." Rae pulled Nikki to her and gave her a big hug.

Something was not right with that hug, not right at all. Nikki sensed the familiar smell of Rae, the scent of the house, the familiar sounds of the street they lived on.

Thunder rolled. Then Nikki remembered Paul.

"No!" Nikki pushed violently back from Rae's embrace. "No! It's not you! It's Paul!"

Rae's grip tightened about Nikki's shoulders. She drew the girl toward her as if preparing to kiss her but as their mouths neared one another, Rae began to gag and choke as a thick, bloody red tentacle snaked its way up her throat and out of the woman's mouth.

Nikki screamed and tried to break the iron grip the woman held on her. Rae's jaws began to split apart to let the massive organ slide from within her. The end of the thrashing obscenity opened to reveal a slavering orifice, itself lined with hundreds of needle- sharp teeth. It snaked about Nikki's face as blood flew from Rae's ripping head and Nikki struggled to master the horror of what she now realized to be an attack of Apollyon.

Rae maintained her grip on the struggling Nikki as the older woman's head split and her body ripped with the sickening sound of someone tearing the material of a window shade. From within Rae there burst a glistening, multi-tentacled creature. A great fleshy sack of ooze, it billowed and pulsated, tentacles whipping the air and the snaky organ darting toward Nikki's face in its attempts to enter her mouth.

As Rae's body ripped and fell away the tentacles which had been within her arms thrashed for

a moment in an attempt to maintain their grip. That was when Nikki found her break.

For a moment the two struggled, then Nikki broke free. Her eyes flashed wildly as she backed away from the creature Rae had become. A queasy feeling crept into her stomach and a cold shudder ran through her.

"No! I won't let this become real!" Nikki turned and bolted out of the house through the kitchen door. As she dashed madly out the door, she stepped immediately on a purple cobblestone sidewalk and stumbled over a shoe shine duck.

"Waaaaarrrggg!" The duck squawked indignantly. "Watch where you're going, you clumsy hairless ape," the duck yelled at Nikki as he picked himself up.

Nikki would have fallen flat on her face had she not been caught by a buffalo in a claw-hammer tuxedo and top hat.

"My dear, do take care dashing about the streets!" The buffalo eyed her through a monacle.

Nikki reeled in horror, pulled from the buffalo's steadying grip, and felt her stomach wrench. Her bathrobe flared about her legs as she began to run. As soon as she'd broken into a run, she was nearly tripped by frogs.

"We're in the money! We're in the money!" The frogs sang and danced in a chorus line across the street.

"Maaaaammy, how I love you, how I love you..." A little black duck was on one knee beside Nikki mimicking Al Jolsen quite convincingly.

Nikki fought the very real need to pass out, then wished she had, as a police gorilla approached her.

"Meow," the police gorilla drawled in an Alabama accent, as he sidled up beside her.

Nikki's face mirrored the expression of someone who had just been offered maggot pudding. She tried to say something but when she opened her mouth the only sound that came from her resembled something not very unlike the sound a turkey never makes. That was the exact description her mind gave it and at the time it seemed to fit the sound very well.

A beaver in trench coat and hat leaned against a lamp post.

"Over here, sweetheart!" The beaver sounded just like Humphrey Bogart.

"Meow," the police gorilla whispered in a sexy voice, right into Nikki's ear.

"Come on, sweetheart, move it." The beaver tossed a cigarette to the pavement, crushing it with his shoe.

"Meow!"

"Mammy, how I love you, how I love you, my dear ol' mammy!"

"We're in the money, we're in the money..."

Nikki walked, turning around and around, her hands to her ears trying to shut out the madness.

The beaver walked toward her.

"Meow," the police gorilla insisted, nuzzling his face against Nikki's.

"Shove off, you big ape!" The beaver pushed past the simian cop.

Nikki staggered; she knew it was well past time for her to faint dead away.

"Come on, toots," the beaver said as he reached out a paw to steady her. "Don't pull the big snooze on me now. What's a nice kid like you doing in a place like this, anyway?"

"Where am I?" Nikki squatted to eye level with the beaver, clapped her hands onto his shoulders. "Who are you? How do I get out of this loony tune world?"

"Easy sister, easy," the beaver replied in a suave voice.

"One thing at a time. First, let's get you off the streets. Somebody is liable to think you're crazy, or me for talking to you."

"What are you talking about? How is th..."

"Not now, toots, not now. Let's get to my office. Here, follow me." The beaver took Nikki by the hand and turned to lead her. She did not know why, but for some reason she followed, maybe because the beaver seemed to be so in control of the situation. At least he seemed to recognize that she did not belong in this world.

"Hi, Mick, how's the family doing?" The beaver tipped his hat as he spoke to a group of mice who passed them. Nikki and the beaver then wound their way down several streets and into an alley.

"I know this may not make much sense to you right now, toots," the beaver began, as he led the way up a flight of rickety stairs on the outside of a grimy office building, "but somebody is looking for you and I have to get you the heck out of town and fast."

They reached the top of the stairs and the beaver produced a key. He unlocked the door that faced them and Nikki found herself looking into a dark doorway.

"Go on in, toots," the beaver said, as he held the door for her. Nikki took one tentative step into the dark, then a second and a third. She heard the door close behind her. Far ahead she could just make out a faint light.

"Mister Beaver?" she nervously called out. "Where are we?"

There was no answer. Quickly she turned back only to find nothing behind her but total blackness, no door, nothing. Then the fear struck again. Nikki spun and began to run. She had no plan or reason. Reason seemed to have long ago taken a vacation. She ran wild and blind toward the distant light. She ran until she felt what seemed to be soft earth beneath her feet. Her legs were slapped by what felt like the limbs of small bushes. They pulled and tore at her bathrobe as on and on she ran, from darkness into a misty twilight.

She screamed as she ran, even though the fear seemed to be falling behind her, and she held her hands to her ears trying to shut out the distant sound of mad pipers which once again made another play for entry into her head. Briars slapped her bare thighs as pieces of terry cloth were shredded from her robe and were left behind on the brush.

She was running down a short hill when she broke from the misty twilight into broad daylight.

At the bottom of the hill flowed a crystal clear brook which splashed her bare legs with icy water as she staggered to a complete halt in its middle.

The brook was about ten feet wide and its opposite shore held the most beautiful land that Nikki had ever dreamed of. She stood for a moment in the shallow brook's water. Her robe hung from her in tatters and she was scratched and streaked with dirt and blood. Her legs stung from the wild lashing the briery bushes had given them. She was beyond thought, beyond reason. She sniffed back a heavy sob and staggered forward to the beautiful shore. She made it to the brook's edge and collapsed into a deep sleep on the soft grassy bank.

CHAPTER VI

The Land of Tir Nan Og

*H*arold surveyed the street of houses he had been led to by the fire in his hands. Slowly he coasted down the sidewalk, reading the steady signal in his burning fingertips. The fire had reached from finger to elbow at this street and for ten minutes he had coasted up and down the block taking readings as the heat of his fingertips changed. He settled on one house where he finally came to a stop.

"Well, what now, Harold old boy?" he asked himself. "I wonder what Krazy Kat would say if he were here? I mean besides 'Meroooowwww,' which is mostly what he says anyway." Somehow joking to himself helped calm the nervousness he felt.

"Well," he finally decided, "I guess he would say I should go up to the door and knock, then ask if Nikki Renn is at home." With that he gathered his resolve, kicked the skateboard up into his hands, and advanced on the door.

He knocked.

A fully reformed Rae opened the door. "Yeah, kid, what do you want?" She sounded anything but happy as she glowered at Harold.

"Excuse me, but I was wondering if Nikki is in? You see, I'm her brother and I've come a very long way to see her."

"What in holy crude are you doing here, kid?"

Rae froze him with her stare. She paused to think for a moment before speaking again. "Well, I guess it doesn't matter much. Nikki is having one of her days, kid. She just got miffed at me and blasted out the back door. I haven't seen her since. Maybe I can tell her you were here."

With that Rae slammed the door in Harold's face.

"Well, *thank you*, Miss America!" Harold shouted after her. "I guess I'll just go around to the backyard and help myself to it. I've got to quit talking to myself," he said to himself nervously.

Harold walked to the side of the house, then between it and the neighboring house to a ten foot high redwood fence which surrounded Rae's backyard.

"Oh nuts, no gate on this side," Harold grumbled. He cast about for a moment before deciding that the garbage can next to Rae's house would be about the right height for him to stand on to see into the backyard. He dropped his skateboard, wrestled the can to the side of the fence and hopped onto it. Reaching for the peaked tops of the fence slats, he pulled himself up high enough to see into the backyard.

There WAS no backyard.

There was nothing. Harold looked into the face of total void — the uncreated.

"Holy spit," Harold stated flatly, in total disbelief. Even after all that had happened today, Harold was still not prepared for what was on the other side of Rae's back fence.

Slowly the teenager lowered himself to the ground. Sitting on the moist earth with his back to the fence, a wild flash of insanity shot through the boy's eyes. For a long moment he sat as if no mind dwelt within him. In fact his mind was still intact, but it swirled with the phantasmagoria of a surrealistic, lunatic cartoon world.

His brain filled with the vision of a creature. It was an almost amorphous blob at first, but slowly it changed into the shape of a head. It reminded Harold of an octopus, with eerily glowing eyes and skin like greenish-black rubber. Its flabby form pulsed like an octopus and its tentacles waved hideously from where the mouth should have been.

Harold saw the head rise like a dark moon over the horizon of a cartoon city, until it filled the night sky. It rolled back to laugh, revealing jagged fanglike teeth in a maw behind the writhing tentacles. As it laughed, a sulfurous smoke rolled from the maw and the sound of mad pipers shrilled through the air. A thousand terrors too deep for the soul of man flooded Harold as the creature laughed, for the boy knew that he was seeing the very face of Apollyon himself, and that the demon was preparing to destroy Nikki.

But even as the vision played before the boy's eyes, a power began to fill his being. It started with the now-familiar warmth in his hands but was soon a fire rushing up his arms toward his heart. The power filled him, lifted him and brought him to a vision apart from the rising face of terror.

Suddenly, Harold saw Nikki spinning round and round in a street full of talking animals, obviously in total confusion. At that moment, Harold felt the fire fill his brain, like a rush of fresh air into the lungs of a suffocating man.

"*Project your thoughts, Harold!*" The voice of Gwydion spoke calmly and with assurance through the fire.

"My thoughts. My thoughts? Yes, that's it!"

Harold's mind whirled but this time with creativity rather than terror. And it was to Bucky Beaver, his favorite childhood cartoon character, that his mind instantly turned.

Harold thought, he projected, he warned, and he watched. He felt the fire leaving him and saw it fill the form of Bucky Beaver. He watched in his mind as the beaver moved, talked, lived.

"Safety," Harold spoke. "Where is safety? Where is any sanity that Apollyon has not touched?"

"*Here, Harold,*" the voice of Gwydion spoke. A spark of the fire burst within the lad's mind like a skyrocket on a July night. For one brief moment a picture flowed from the mind of Gwydion to Harold. It was a picture of the most beautiful land

Harold had ever seen, a land of golden trees and unspoiled beauty.

"*Yes, there!*" his answering thought shouted. His mind and power guided him and he watched Nikki, saw her running, saw her fall in exhaustion on the far shore of a clear stream.

He blinked and once again found himself sitting against the fence of Rae's un-backyard. He jumped to his feet.

"I know where you are, Nikki Elaine Renn!" He kicked the skateboard into his hands. "And I know how to get there!"

Harold raced back to the front yard and up to the door of Rae's house. He banged on the door with a passion. Within the house he heard footsteps coming. He banged again.

"Okay, okay, I'm coming. You don't have to bang the door down!" Rae flung the door open. "Hey, kid, what in the world..."

"Gang way, Godzilla!" Harold burst past Rae and into her living room.

"Hey, get back here, I don't care if you are Nikki's brother," Rae shouted after the boy as he flashed passed her into the hall.

Harold spun for the kitchen, saw the backdoor standing open with swirling nothingness beyond. He dropped the skateboard to the floor and his feet hit it full force. A healthy kick-off sent him flying toward the eternity of non-being before him.

"Darn you, kid, get out of my house with that skateboard!" Rae stormed up the hallway as Harold shot through the backdoor and into a free-fall that took him into the void between all the might-have-beens that could have ever existed.

* * *

The smell of fresh flowers awoke Nikki from the first good sleep she'd had since beginning her adventure. Now her mind was fogged with the lingering effects of sleep and outrageous events, and she thought at first that she was at home and in her own bed. As she stirred in an attempt to snuggle her way deeper into the fresh smelling sheets she felt the soft grass about her body.

Her mind awoke. Nikki bolted upright in the grass. She had been moved a few yards from the stream bank and was lying beneath a grove of flowering trees. She was completely nude and the tattered bath robe was folded and lay a few feet from her. Her legs no longer stung but were marked with red welts where the thorny brush had lashed her.

"Do not be startled," a gentle voice spoke from behind her. "I treated your wounds with salve and have been watching over you since I found you lying by the brook."

At the sound of the voice, Nikki sprung around with the nimbleness of a cat. She crouched, feet wide, fingertips resting lightly on the grass, ready to spring on a moment's notice. Her hair was loose over her shoulders and several locks fell onto her face, giving her quite a feral look in such sylvan surroundings.

"I am Eilian," said the most beautiful girl Nikki had ever seen in her life. "I am of the Tylwyth Teg. You are in the land of Tir Nan Og where Gwyn ap Nudd is king. Across the Eastern Sea, in Tirfo Thuinn, Fin Bheara rules over our sister people, the Tuatha de Danann. Together our lands make up the world of Elfame, the Shores Beyond Time."

The girl stood as she spoke. She wore only a short garment, the lightest wisp of diaphanous yellow gossamer. This was draped over her right shoulder and hung down her front and back to just below her hips where the corners were gathered at the hip and fastened with a golden leaf-shaped pin. What little of the girl's body it covered shimmered through as if being seen within a golden light. On her feet were golden sandals.

Slowly Nikki rose to stand.

"I'm Nikki Renn," was all she could think to say at the moment. She still stood in a wide defensive stance. She shook the locks back from her face. "I do not know where I am," she said, finding her words. "But I know I am darned tired of being scared and intimidated. I am not going to let myself be the victim of every lunatic and demonic force in the universe anymore. If you are here to run some kind of number on me I'll just say this, I may go down but you're in for one heck of a fight!"

"You are of the Daughters-of-Man, are you not, Nikkirenn?" Eilian asked.

"What are you talking about, 'Daughters-of-Man'?" Nikki shifted her weight slightly from one foot to the other, anticipating an attack at any moment.

"I am what you would call fairy-folk," Eilian continued. "We know the same Creator as you and once dwelt within the Shores of Time as you. Some of our folk became evil, that was many ages ago, and, well, it is too long a story to tell here and now. We left your lands and now dwell here."

"Great, I ended up in *Disneyland*," Nikki said, shifting to a more relaxed position.

"What is this *Disneyland*?" Eilian asked.

"Oh, nothing." Nikki now managed a smile to Eilian. "Just a weak attempt at humor in the face of the insane. My little brother does it a lot better." For some reason Harold seemed to be heavily on her mind at the moment.

"I have spun you a garment while you slept." Eilian returned Nikki's smile as she stooped and lifted a gossamer garment like her own from the grass. It was such a perfect green that Nikki had failed to see it against the bright blades.

She walked over to Nikki and draped the sheer cloth over Nikki's right shoulder, tying it at the hip for lack of a clip. It felt light as a spring breeze and filled Nikki with a nostalgic peace and confidence. It was the same feeling she'd had as a little girl when her mother would pick her up and hold her tight. At those times she had felt like nothing in the world had the power to hurt her. The fairy-garment gave her that same childlike peace.

"Let us go to my people," Eilian said as she adjusted Nikki's gossamer garment. The garment made Nikki's body shimmer through its greenness, giving her nude form the look of innocence Eve must have had when she stood within the Garden with only the aura of her own innocence as clothing. Where the fabric fell across her body it clung like spider silk and in spite of its scantness it gave her an overall feeling of warmth.

"You will be welcome among my people as a Daughter-of-Man and we will be eager to hear the story of what brings you to our Shores Beyond Time."

Eilian took Nikki by the hand and led the way. Nikki followed, feeling for the first time since the beginning of her adventure that something made sense. She was not sure what it was, but she knew it was so.

"It feels like Indian summer back home," she commented as the two began walking through the golden grove. "There is the smell and feel of autumn in the air but it's as warm as spring."

"It is always like this in our land," Eilian said. She let go of Nikki's hand and knelt into the lush grass where a large patch of violets grew. She began plucking them and weaving them into a chain.

Nikki shifted from foot to foot, anxious to get on to Eilian's people, but the fairy-girl seemed totally absorbed in the flowers at the moment.

"Shouldn't we be hurrying? I wouldn't want to be stuck in the woods at night."

"Oh, there is no need to hurry." Eilian looked up from her flower weaving with a smile. "Time as you know it has little meaning here in Tir Nan Og."

She looked back to her work, made a few more loops with the violets and joined them into a perfect circle.

"Here." Eilian rose to her feet and held the flowers out to Nikki. "I've made you a present. It's a circlet for your hair."

The fairy reached out and placed the circlet on Nikki's head, then stood back to admire it.

"You are very beautiful, Daughter-of-Man," she said, after a moment.

Nikki blushed. She had just been thinking that the fairy was the most beautiful person she had ever seen in her life. To be told that she was beautiful by someone as radiant as Eilian seemed somehow very inept.

"I don't understand," Nikki replied, giving Eilian a puzzled look. "How can you think I am beautiful? I'm just an ordinary girl. But you, now you would certainly turn all the guys' heads at home."

Eilian threw back her head and the woods came alive with her laughter. It was a musical laughter which rang through the woods like silver bells, and bespoke a joy springing from a depth of which man could only dream.

Nikki giggled like a little girl as a shudder of happiness passed through her. Eilian looked at her and the joy in the fairy's eyes made Nikki want to shout and dance about amongst the trees.

"I feel like dancing." She giggled again as she spoke to the fairy.

"Yes!" Eilian shouted in joy. "Let's dance!" And with that, the fairy grabbed Nikki's hands and they began to dance about like schoolgirls in the lush grass beneath the ever-golden trees of Tir Nan Og.

They danced and whirled, hand in hand under the trees until Nikki lost all sense of direction and time. When they finally stopped they fell in a laughing pile of arms and legs.

"I have never felt so happy and free in my entire life," Nikki said, pulling herself upright to sit with her back to the gigantic tree. "But still, I don't see how you could think me beautiful. I mean, if you are any example of what your people look like you leave us a long way behind."

The fairy sprang up, danced a little pirouette and flashed a heart-melting smile at Nikki.

"It is because you reflect the beauty of our Creator, Nikkirenn, Daughter-of-Man," Eilian replied. She then spun another pirouette and dashed like lightning behind a tree.

In a moment she popped back out, a pixie grin on her face. "I'll tell you a story." She popped behind the tree again only to pop out on the other side almost immediately. "If you have the time," she continued, popping back and out again in a flash of golden light, "in this land Beyond The Shores of Time."

Nikki smiled at her. Not only was this the most beautiful person Nikki had ever met in her life, she was also the most radiantly cheerful.

Eilian stepped to the side of the tree, placed her face against the smooth bark and wrapped her arms around the trunk. A smile stayed on the fairy's face, but her eyes took on a far away aspect, as if she were looking back through all the ages of time.

"My story begins so long ago, my mind fades into the mists of eternity as I try to remember; yet again it is almost as if it happened yesterday."

As the fairy spoke, her voice carried Nikki away to a world before the establishment of what the Daughter-of-Man would call Time. It was as if a spell were woven and she not only heard the words as Eilian spoke them, but she could see the events played out before her eyes.

"When all was created and made perfect," the fairy began, "El Elyon created the mighty four to guard his creation — Michael, Gabriel, Raphael and Uriel, the mighty Archangels who hold the four corners of creation. There were worlds made within worlds, dimensions beyond dimensions and planets upon planets and it was deemed wise by El Elyon to create for himself one to oversee it all. This one would report only to El Elyon himself and none other in all of creation would be above him.

"This mighty one was called the Anointed Cherub That Covereth, and he was the most powerful and beautiful being of all the handiworks of El Elyon. The Anointed Cherub was given a throne second only to that of El Elyon and it was placed on the world which you call Earth, and was located within the dimension which you call Time.

"For untold ages the Earth was ruled in peace and flowered as the most beautiful planet of the entire multi universe. My people were placed there to tend it and we answered directly to the Anointed Cherub as stewards of the Earth. All went according to the grand plan of El Elyon, until that black day, the day that evil was born.

"It began as a seed of envy in the heart of the Anointed Cherub but it grew quickly. He decided that he rightfully should rule all the worlds of the multi universe and he began to tell lies that many of our people believed. We had followed him since the day of our creation, and it was hard for us to believe that he would lead us into something that was not right and good. But some of us did not believe him. We knew that the will of El Elyon could not be moved against. We tried to stop the Anointed Cherub and war broke out.

"We were vastly outnumbered, for not only did most of the races that dwelt upon the Earth follow the Anointed Cherub, but a third of the fiery spirits who had followed Michael and the others of the mighty four joined the Anointed Cherub. The war raged on for hundreds of years. The mighty four sent aid to us but in the end, Earth was blasted to cinders by the Cherub and his rebel army.

"We would all have died had not El Elyon himself stepped in himself and blasted the rebels with the fiery breath of his judgement. We who did not fall watched the re-creation of the Earth and the rise of man. For centuries we lived amongst you, until you became too numerous. It was then, when there were not forest and glen enough for us that we moved to Tir Nan Og, Beyond the Shores of Time.

"Those of our people who fell became crea-tures of darkness — hobgoblins, bogies, Red Caps and other evil beings who haunt both your world and ours. The Anointed Cherub was doomed to live as a wraith of evil upon your Earth until the end of Time. There he tempts the hearts of men to test and approve them for life everlasting or damnation eternal. I believe the Sons-of-Man now call him the

Devil. All the fallen spirits who once followed the mighty four in service to El Elyon became demons and devils. Many had become so ultimately evil that El Elyon had to banish them to the Abyss Beyond Time, least they destroy creation utterly and immediately. The Devil swore to find a way to release them so that he could destroy creation and get revenge against El Elyon. The mightiest of those insane imprisoned spirits is called Apollyon. It is he who lead early man to destruction in the days of Noah, and it is he the Devil Cherub most wishes to release."

"What?" Nikki sprang to her feet. "That's who I'm fighting! That's who was after me when I was running and found myself in your world!"

"No!" Eilian stepped from the tree, distress taking control of her face. "Apollyon is loosed? He could destroy all that is if he is not stopped!"

"He already has destroyed my entire universe." Nikki felt the urgency of her mission return. "And Paul and I, that's my boyfriend, and Gwydion, he's a big white cat, and Old Joshua, who is really a gryphon named Counselor, and one other person we're not sure who it is, are supposed to find a way to defeat him and bring a might-have-been back to replace our universe."

"If what you say is true," Eilian said, grabbing Nikki by the hand, "then even my world is in danger. We must hurry to my people and let the king hear of this. He will know what to do."

Eilian knelt and untied the golden sandals from her feet, stood and gave them to Nikki.

"Here, Nikkirenn, put these on quickly. We must make all possible haste and my sandals will give you speed your feet do not know."

Nikki hesitated for a moment. The fairy-sandals looked too small for her by at least a size, but when she placed them on her feet, to her surprise they were a perfect fit. She quickly tied them on, then Eilian took her by the hand and they were off through the woods like golden shadows on the wind.

"I thought you said time had no meaning here," Nikki reminded the fairy as they ran.

"It usually doesn't. It only does when an archdemon is bent on destroying creation!"

They left the golden grove where Eilian had found Nikki asleep on the bank of the brook. Into a rolling meadowland they ran. Nikki was in awe of the beauty of the land. Never had she seen such fields of grass and flowers, and the trees which were spotted here and there glimmered the same golden green as the woods where she awoke.

Time had ceased to have meaning to Nikki. She could not tell if they had run for hours or weeks, and she and the fairy spoke little as they ran. She noticed that no matter how long they ran, she did not grow tired. Finally night began to fall and as twilight approached, a new woods came into sight ahead of them. Nightfall found them entering the woods and as the darkness coaxed the last bits of twilight from the world, Nikki marveled at what she saw. Around them it seemed that thousands of fireflies were dancing in the air. They zipped and dipped through the trees, shedding a sparkling glow wherever they went.

Nikki broke the long silence. "What are all those fireflies?"

"Those are Pixie folk, they will do us no harm. But you must beware of their evil kin, Will-O-The-Wisps; they always mislead," the fairy returned.

Eilian slowed their pace to a fast trot.

"The village of my people lies not far ahead," she said "We will be..."

She did not finish before the brush to their left came alive with the most horrid bellowing and crying, and through the brush burst the most grotesquely misformed figure of a cow that Nikki could ever have imagined. The cow looked as if it had been starved by evil farmers for at least ten years. Its eyes glowed a pale yellow and little flames flickered from its mouth and nostrils.

Nikki screamed and leapt backward into a large raspberry bush. The grotesque cow bounded past Eilian and pranced around Nikki, shaking its emaciated head, swishing its mangy tail and laughing so hard, in a very human voice, that tears rolled from its glowing eyes.

"Headley Kow, I know your name so begone ye bogie beast, afore I tell it to all this company present and ye lose your power in this wood!" Eilian cried at the creature, finger outstretched toward the prancing, laughing bogie beast.

"Eilian of Tylwyth Teg," the creature called back in the cackling voice of a story book witch, "I'll be gone indeed but first I'll make poo-poo on your little friend from the Fields of Man!"

"You'll be gone now ye bogie beast or I'll call your true name for sure!" Eilian took one step closer to the bogie, a deadly seriousness in her eyes. As she did so, Nikki managed to pull herself from the raspberry bush.

"I've been frightened out of my wits for the last time!" she cried at the beast. "If you were some monster I might be afraid, but you're not!"

Nikki's blood was boiling. "Faker!" she cried. "You might have caught me off guard and frightened me but now I know that's all you are, a no good mischievous faker!"

"No fair!" the beast shrieked and drew back. "No fair and nasty play! You said you would not call my name if I leave but Daughter-of-Man shrieks it out for all the nasty Pixies to hear!"

"What?" Nikki looked at Eilian in confusion but the fairy was holding a hand up for her to keep silence.

"You pick the wrong one to play your tricks on tonight beast," Eilian said to the creature who was now sitting in a very sulky position, its head hung almost to the ground in a deep pout. "This is Nikkirenn, the one of all the Daughters-of-Man chosen to destroy Apollyon. She knows the names of all your kind but to show kindness she will not banish you with the Final Word."

At those words the beast jumped up and took up its cocky grin once again.

"Go now, tell all those of your kind to beware if they ever see the Daughter-of-Man called Nikkirenn for surely she will banish you all with the naming of your true names!"

With that the beast laughed a maniacal laugh and bounded off into the brush leaving nothing but the echo of its laughter behind.

Eilian turned to Nikki.

"How did you know its name!" she asked.

"I didn't. What do you mean?" Nikki returned.

"You named its true name, *Faker*, thus you had total power over it. You did not know that?" Eilian asked.

"I had no idea," Nikki said, looking off in the direction the bogie beast had vanished. "What was that thing anyway?"

"Oh, just a Headley Kow, nothing important. They are a degenerate form of our own Gwartheg Y Llyn, fairy-cattle. They cause a lot of mischief, especially if they roam into the Shores of Time where they love to catch travelers at night, frighten them, and usually chase them until they fall victim into a mud hole or brook or something. Then they prance around laughing and dash off into the woods. I guess he thought he would pull it on you."

"Yeah? Well I'm tired of having every two-bit creep in the universe pull its number on me. From now on this kid's fighting back," Nikki returned.

"I am sure that is why you were chosen to battle Apollyon." Eilian turned and took Nikki's hand again. "Come, we are near my home."

Through the trees and brush they proceeded for a while longer until they heard music. It sounded to Nikki like a fiddle and pipes. After a moment lights could be seen through the trees.

"There is the sithein of my people." Eilian pointed to a small clearing which was opening before them.

The first thing Nikki noticed were the fairy-folk — and there were hundreds of them. They were dancing, singing, cooking, eating, drinking and celebrating in every way possible. Fiddlers fiddled, pipers piped and dancers danced. Everyone was busy with merriment of one sort or another. Nikki became so excited that she boldly stepped from the woods.

The moment she set foot in the clearing everything went perfectly quiet. Lights went out, music stopped and everyone vanished in the twinkling of an eye. There was nothing to be seen but a great grassy mound at the center of an empty clearing.

Nikki looked about in bewilderment as Eilian's laughter rolled behind her.

"Come out, my people!" Eilian called as she stepped from the wood. "I bring a friend from the Daughters-of-Man."

Lights began coming back on and people appeared as if they were stepping from within the trees themselves. Glowing wisps of pastel light floated in the air or rested on the points of branches and pixies dazzled the air with their sparkling glow.

Nikki had thought Eilian beautiful and now she was faced with an entire village of folk just like the fairy-lass. The magic in the air crackled about Nikki's head like electricity as the wonderland of the Fairy came to life around her.

The music slowly picked up again and talk began to fill the air, a sweet language like a music unto itself. Others began to dance again and laughter rang like crystal chimes through and about the trees.

Fairies began to gather about Nikki, each glowing with a faint golden aura of magic. Never had she seen so many smiles of heartfelt joy as they reached out tentative hands to touch her. Sparkling pixies flitted about her head, and one beautiful little pink creature flitted close like a hummingbird, and kissed her on the cheek.

"Welcome, Daughter-of-Man," they said, one after another, as they gathered about her. Fairy-women and fairy-men both crowded in to pay their respects.

"I am honored to be among you," Nikki spoke in return to one after another. Then she said to Eilian, "I don't think I've ever seen such a beautiful and friendly people in my life."

Everyone, both men and women, wore the same simple diaphanous gown draped about them that Eilian and Nikki wore. Their shimmering colors mingled with the werelights and soft Pixie sparkle to create a true wonderland. As Nikki took in all the beauty and friendship, speaking to one after another of the fairy-people, a tall beautiful man of the fairy-kind dressed in golden gossamer and wearing a laurel of golden leaves upon his head approached.

"Our chief approaches, Nikki," Eilian indicated the tall golden man. "I will now introduce you to him and he shall judge your story."

"Ho, Daughter-of-Man," he said, with a voice of golden honey. "What passes in the Fields of Man must be dire indeed for you to be brought here amongst us." He took Nikki's hand as he spoke and, bowing a deep bow, he kissed it.

Nikki tingled as his lips touched her hand. It was a beautiful tingle, as if a ray of pure joy had just been shot through her entire being. For a moment she was breathless, speechless.

"I am honored." She trembled with excitement as she finally found her voice. "But I am afraid that nothing passes within the Fields of Man now, good or bad. That's why I'm here. Apollyon has destroyed our world!"

No sooner had the name passed her lips than silence struck the entire company. It was punctuated by what sounded like a collective gasp, and werelights and pixie sparkle vanished. The whole company was left in the light of the naked stars which filtered through the majestic bows of the wood.

"I see." The fairy-chief broke the long silence. His right hand swept a gesture above his head and the werelights flickered back on, Pixies began peeping from bush and trees. "The tale you have for us is more dire than I ever suspected."

"Hear the words of Ossian your chief," he called out to those gathered about him. "I shall sit in council beside my lovely Niam of the Golden Hair and we shall listen to the words of the Daughter-of-Man. From her words shall we judge what is required of our people."

With that he turned toward the great mound which stood in the center of the clearing.

"Let the Sithein of the people be opened!" he cried. Suddenly a crack formed from top to bottom in the great mound. Light burst from within as the crack widened and the sides of the hillock began to swing outward as if on hinges.

Nikki gasped as she saw a great pillared hall appear within what had seemed only a grass-covered mound. Light flooded from the great hall and she could just make out the form of a woman standing in the doorway.

"Let the people of Tylwyth Teg take council!" Ossian called out to his people. Then to Nikki he said, "Come with me Nikkirenn, Daughter-of-Man. Tonight you shall tell a new thing to a folk who are older than time."

Ossian lead the procession into the great hall of the Sithein of the Tylwyth Teg with Nikki and Eilian at his right and left. Inside, the hall was vast. It seemed, as Nikki entered, to be much larger on the inside than the mound was from the outside.

The Sithein reminded Nikki of pictures of medieval castles she had seen in books. The walls were hung with tapestries woven with great skill. Weapons and armor stood along the walls in stands and braziers blazed bright with fires. Great oak tables and chairs were set as if for a feast and at the far end of the great hall two thrones sat side by side on a raised dias. Doors lead to places Nikki could only wonder at but by now she had begun to assume that the Sithein could hold an infinite number of rooms and halls.

The company moved to the assembly area before the dias and there Ossian joined the woman Nikki had seen standing in the great hall as the doors to the Sithein opened. She was no doubt the most beautiful of all the Tylwyth Teg, if such a thing were possible, and together they seated themselves on the two thrones.

The company gathered before the dias and assembled in order as if by rank. Eilian and Nikki were invited by a wave of Ossian's hand to stand upon the dias before the company. When all were in their places, Ossian stood to speak.

"People of the Tylwyth Teg," he began but he was not allowed to finish for before another word could come from his mouth the air was split by a flash of blue lightning and a peal of thunder threatened to deafen all within the great hall.

The lightening bolt split the air like a curtain being drawn back, and for a moment, Nikki saw the back door of Rae's house appear in the great hall near the feasting tables. Through the door she could see the kitchen from where she had fled earlier. Then she saw Harold, flying from the door on his skateboard. Harold seemed to shimmer as he left the door, then Rae's door and kitchen disappeared. As the thunder clap subsided Harold came sailing up the stone floor of Ossian's great hall on his skateboard and stopped right in front of the dias.

Harold kicked the skateboard into his hands and looked about at the company of fairies gathered about him and at his sister on the dias.

"Hi, Nikki," the boy finally spoke. "Boy are you ever hard to catch up with!"

CHAPTER VII

The Sword, the Horn and the Garter

"*R*amph! Mmeeerrrraowph!"

One of the Cait Sidth's big white paws, claws unextended, swatted briskly at Paul's face. The soft buffeting stirred the drowsy young man.

"Wha...huh?" Paul stirred from a dream.

"Meramph! Fitssss, Reaow!" The big cat bowed and spat, prancing in circles in front of the antique cordovan couch where Paul had fallen asleep.

"Oh, Gwydion." Sleep began to clear from Paul's head. "I'm sorry, I must have fallen asleep." He sat up, rubbing his eyes.

"Merph!" The Cait Sidth turned and bounded toward the stairway, then stopped and turned back to Paul who was still rubbing his eyes. "MERPH!!!" he exclaimed insistently, then turned again and bounded up the stairs.

"I'm coming, I'm coming." Paul was now up and shambling across the floor, clearing the numbness of sleep from his brain. As he reached the door to the stairway he heard Gwydion's heavy galloping halfway up the stairwell.

"Meor-oow!" The cry carried down to where Paul was just starting his climb.

"Yes, I'm coming!" he called back, and when sleep had finally retreated into the deep reaches of his head he remembered Nikki. Paul bounded up the stairs, now carried by a sudden burst of energy. He passed the Cait Sidth who rushed to catch up and together they dashed into the wizard's room at the top of the long stairwell.

"Merrrrow!" Gwydion yowled, as he shot into the ancient library. One great bound carried him from the door to the tabletop, over which Old Joshua now hovered, studying a scattered group of old and arcane books.

"What is it," Paul gasped as he entered. "Did you find Nikki? Has Harold found her yet?"

"No, but don't be in anguish, my friend," Joshua comforted, as the boy rushed to the old man's side. "Gwydion has been in contact with Harold since you fell asleep. We believe that everything is going as well as we could have anticipated."

"Merph!" Gwydion said, as he jumped from the table to a chair by the stained glass window.

"Yes, you get on with things and I'll tell him what I've been reading," Joshua replied, as the cat took possession of his new seat. The old man returned to Paul. "I have come across an old legend which Gwydion and I believe to be of great importance. I must admit to a failure of my memory, for I once knew of the story but somehow had forgotten it.

"Interestingly, Gwydion tells me the same forgetfulness overcame him. Anyway, when I discovered the legend anew a few hours ago, we both remembered it."

"Well, what is it?" A knot of excitement grew in Paul's chest.

"It's the story of True Thomas, that is Thomas the Rhymer or Thomas Rhymer of Erceldoune." Joshua paused to reach across the table for his long-stemmed pipe. "Would you please hand me that pouch beside you, Paul? Thank you."

142

Paul took the pouch Joshua had indicated from a bookshelf and handed it to the old man, who opened it and began stuffing his pipe. He lit the pipe, puffed a few blue smoke rings and contemplated their rising for a moment. "Ahem, where were we, Paul?" The venerable fellow seemed to gaze off into a far past before continuing.

"It seems that Thomas the Rhymer was a poet and something of a prophet in the thirteenth century, and he spent not a short time in the land known as Tir Nan Og, or Elfame. Even though Thomas was a Son-of-Man, like you, his pure heart attracted Dana, the Queen of Elfame, and she invited him to spend time in her kingdom as an honored guest."

He paused again to puff out several dark blue smoke rings. The old man relaxed into an armchair and watched the rings float about the colored light of the room.

"Well, it happened," he said, after the moment's contemplation, "that during Thomas' sojourn in the magical Elfame, the evil spirit lord known to you as the Devil made an attack on that fair land. While Gwyn ap Nudd, who is king of Tir Nan Og and husband of Dana, gathered his warriors to battle the armies of Red Caps and hobgoblins amassed by the powers of evil, Dana delivered Thomas back to the Shores of Time in order to keep him safe." The old man's eyes twinkled at Paul as he said, "Of course, that is your world I'm speaking of, my boy."

He leaned forward and knocked his pipe into a large clay bowl, which rested on a table between the young man and the gentleman. Blue smoke rose from the falling ashes and Joshua circled his hand over the smoke. As he did so, the amount of smoke rising from the clay bowl increased until a great cloud was formed just above its rim.

"*Ecte nolanay coustanelay,*" Joshua spoke and the smoke opened as a curtain. Perfect pictures of the world Joshua described formed above the bowl.

"Oh, man, far out!" Paul marveled, and leaned forward to get a better look at the amazing sight.

"In the old days they called it scrying; I believe you call it a hologram today." The old man smiled at Paul's look of disbelief. "It's really a very simple matter — you just have to know how to induce the electron flow to bend and refract available light rays. The smoke is perfect for that, and presto! You have an instant 3-D TV. So now just sit back and watch as I tell you the tale."

Without taking his eyes from the scenes being played out before him in the smoke of the bowl, Paul pulled a chair toward the small table. He sat forward and propped his elbows on the table to get a better look.

While Joshua recounted his story, in the enchanted smoke Paul saw pictures of noble fairy-warriors atop the ramparts of a majestic castle, fighting hideously ugly creatures of darkness. Then the scene changed, and the fighting was on a vast plane with great armored warriors astride barded fairy-horses, leading charges against seemingly insurmountable numbers of servants of the dark lord. The war raged until it seemed the dark powers would totally overthrow the forces of good.

"On and on the war raged," intoned Joshua over the epic scenes being played out in the smoke, "until the forces of evil were very near to victory. It was then that Gwyn ap Nudd called to the King of Heaven for aid. And so, for the second time since their making, the Creator heard the cry of that race of good and beautiful people, and He blasted the armies of the evil one before they could destroy those whom your people call "the Fairies."

Now the picture in the smoke showed the sky rolled back like a scroll, and from out of the heavens charged an army of white-clothed warriors mounted on white horses and wielding flaming swords. They engaged the armies of evil, making short work of them. As the last ones were being put to the sword, the smoke cleared away and the picture faded from Paul's sight.

For long moments silence reigned. Paul was first to disturb the quiet. "Incredible!"

"Yes." Joshua relit his pipe. "And there's more to the story still. The people you call fairies or elves are the last of a race which vastly predates man on this Earth. They also happen to be the only ones of that race who did not turn evil when the one you call the Devil instigated a great civil war against the rule of El Elyon, the Creator of all. On that early occasion as on this one, the great archangel Michael lead the armies of the Creator to battle against the forces of evil.

"And after this second event of deliverance by the might of the Creator, Michael announced to the fairy-king that he would have to pay a price. 'Choose for yourself one hundred of your finest warriors,' Michael told Gwyn ap Nudd. 'And they shall be hidden away in a secret place by El Elyon. Twice have you been saved from total destruction because you have refused to follow the path of evil, but there shall come a third time when evil will seem to have victory in its grasp. On that day shall you rise up for the salvation of all!' And with that, Michael and all his mighty army rode back into the skies and the clouds rolled back into their courses behind them."

"Tell me about the warriors Gwyn ap Nudd picked," Paul urged, as Joshua paused to puff more smoke rings.

"Well," the old man said, reaching across the scatter of books to one particular tome which he drew to himself. He puffed some more as he flipped through the book. "It says right here that a council was held in the court of the king where it was decided that none other than the king's personal guard would suffice for the job. There were ninety-nine of them, with the hundredth being their leader, one by the name of Artus, who had once lived within the Shores of Time upon a divinely inspired mission to aid the Sons-of-Man."

Old Joshua shifted in his chair again, his eyes twinkling at Paul. "Yes, and you might think you recognize the root name for your famous King Arthur there and you are right," he continued. "For the King Arthur of legend was none other than the great Artus himself, warrior in service to Gwyn ap Nudd. Anyway, what happened next is a bit obscure but from the best sources, I gather that Michael himself spirited away the mighty one hundred and left them sleeping within a hidden mound. They will be roused when Michael's third prophecy Michael's occurs, and they can only be roused by a Son-of-Man.

"There are three items which guard the warriors — a stone sword, a horn, and a garter. Only a
Son-of-Man can draw the stone sword from its sheath
and cut the garter, then blow the horn. When that
is done the warriors will arise as if from the dead
and on that day they will ride into battle against the
powers of evil for the salvation of all."

"But you started by telling me about True Thomas. What does he have to do with your story, and
with Nikki?" Paul asked, as Joshua paused once
again.

"Ah, I'm just getting to that." Joshua reached
for another ancient book. He thumbed through it
for a moment.

"Oh, yes, here we are," he said, continuing
with his tale. "Thomas spent some years back in his
homeland. He became a poet of great renown, settled
in Erceldoune and for many years enjoyed life there.
He never forgot his life in Tir Nan Og, however,
and one night when he was giving a feast in his
castle a man ran into the feast with the report that
two deer had just run from the forest and were
walking through the streets of the town."

"Don't tell me," Paul guessed. "They were fairy-
deer?"

"Well, according to this one story they must
have been," Joshua answered. "For Thomas be-

came very excited at the news and ran from the feast into the street. He found the deer, who seemed to recognize him, and they immediately led him from the town and into the wood. Thomas was never seen within the lands of man again."

"So how does all this tie together? So far we have two very interesting stories but I don't see any connection between Thomas and the sleeping warriors," Paul said.

"Meerrrr. Meerrrr. Merph-reow." Gwydion burbled from deep within his chest. The Cait Sidth sat like an ivory statue in the chair, flooded by the light from the stained glass.

"Now, what do you suppose he has found?" Joshua asked, ignoring Paul's question for the moment. He got up and went to the chair where the big white cat sat. "Gwydion, what is it? What do you see?"

The big cat sat as still as if it were carved from stone. Joshua held a hand above the cat's head, closed his eyes and concentrated for a moment.

"He is in contact with Harold!" The old man turned to Paul with the news. "It seems Nikki is in some predicament. I can't tell exactly what the trouble is."

"Isn't there anything we can do to help?" Paul asked, his face drawn with worry for Nikki.

"Gwydion is in contact and can offer advice, but other than that, we can only wait and see."

He returned to his seat by Paul.

"Sit down, my young friend," Joshua said, taking his seat. "Gwydion is an old hand at things like this. Nikki and Harold are getting the best help available right now."

Paul sat back down but his face still reflected his anxiety.

"Here," Joshua said, reaching for yet another book. "You wanted to know how the stories of True Thomas and the sleeping warriors tie in.

"It seems, from this book, that Thomas indeed returned to Tir Nan Og and that because he was a Son-of-Man and of such a pure heart, the king entrusted to him the job of keeping the horses of the sleeping warriors." Joshua paused a moment for effect. "It is he alone who knows the location of the mound beneath which the warriors sleep."

Joshua sat back with a smile of satisfaction, his story obviously complete.

"But I still don't get it," Paul protested. "I don't see any significance in the story. What does it have to do with us and our problem?"

"Can't you see, my boy?" Joshua leaned forward and pushed one of the books toward Paul, his finger on a passage. "The third time of Michael's prophecy — what we call the third day — this has got to be it!"

Paul shook his head.

"Paul, Gwydion and I both believe that we are in that third day of prophecy. We believe that this entire attack of Apollyon's is that time when the sleeping warriors are to pay back their debt to The Father. On the third day they will rise for the salvation of all!"

The light of realization wiped the worry from Paul's face.

"The sleeping warriors!" His fist hit the table. "They are the ones who can defeat Apollyon and we have got to find them!"

＊　＊　＊

"This is an astounding story you have related to us," Ossian spoke to Nikki and Harold, who still wore his jeans and tee shirt, after politely refusing the gossamer toga which had been offered to him. The two sat at the chief's right hand at high table. "I can hardly believe that the Fields of Man have been destroyed."

The feast to honor the Children-of-Man had continued the entire Elfame night, but how long that measured in time, neither Nikki nor Harold could tell. Both had become oblivious to the passage of time as they were used to. The night could have lasted years, or only hours.

"What can your people do to help us defeat the demon Apollyon?" Harold asked.

"Eilian said we should perhaps go to the king," his sister added. Nikki wore a beautiful short sari of deep blue gossamer, as fine and thin as spider's silk.

"To the king indeed," Ossian returned. "This story you bring us is also of the utmost importance to our people. If Apollyon had truly broken from his prison, then the threat to our own world is very dire. We shall send you off to the king with the coming of dawn. Surely he will know what to do. You two rest now, and we shall begin preparations for your journey."

With a clap of Ossian's hands the gathered fairy-folk arose from all around the feasting tables and began to busy themselves preparing food and baggage for the journey.

"I shall send Eilian with you. She is the one who brought you here and I believe that she should continue with you on your journey," Ossian added, as he escorted the two from the feasting hall. Eilian followed close behind.

"I will also send Fionn. He is the best fighter of this sithein, and who knows what Red Caps or bogies you may meet on the way."

"Eilian, show Nikki and Harold to their beds now," Ossian directed to the fairy-girl. Then to the teenagers he added, "We shall fetch you from your rest when the time for your departure is nigh."

Harold had not realized how tired he really was until Ossian mentioned sleep, and then suddenly he felt as if he had not slept in a lifetime. Nikki, too, stretched and yawned as Eilian lead them away from the feast hall and into their adjoining bed chambers, both of which were hung with beautiful heavy tapestries and appointed with exquisite fairy-wrought furniture. Each of their lushly canopied beds were filled with goosedown and covered with fine silk sheets. The two were fast asleep by the time their heads hit the goosedown pillows.

Fairy-chimes ringing through the sithein's halls roused Harold and Nikki from dreams of sunny Elfame, and the two arose quickly, eager to begin their journey to the castle of Gwyn ap Nudd. They helped themselves to fresh pitchers of hot cider, which Eilian brought to their bed chambers. The spicy cider cleared the sleep from their minds and tingled them with renewed strength and vitality.

After several cups of the cider, Harold was sent to wash up and help with the last preparations for their journey. Eilian took Nikki to a carved marble sauna and bath, where the Daughter-of-Man bathed herself in naturally hot water which bubbled from underground springs. To Nikki's delight, the water was scented with myrrh and it tingled her skin all over. When she got out of the water, she found that the cuts on her legs from the mad dash through the thorn bushes were completely healed.

After Nikki dried herself, Eilian returned with several packages. "I have brought you presents from Ossian and Niam," the fairy-girl said as she entered. "It is hoped they will help you on your way."

"Presents?" Nikki rushed to see what Eilian would draw from the packages which she was now opening.

The first item she brought out was a short gossamer garment, the most elegant Nikki had seen since her arrival in Tir Nan Og. Nikki quickly slipped it over her head. It was made like a poncho, with an opening for the head but no side seams. It hung loosely over her body, falling just to the tops of her thighs. Eilian then withdrew a wide golden belt and with it she encircled Nikki's waist, lacing it together in the front. Nikki's body shimmered through the thin white light of the fabric with a magic which would drive even the most lascivious thought from the mind of anyone who beheld her.

"This is perfect! It's so beautiful," Nikki said, as Eilian finished lacing the golden girdle. "I feel so strong and secure now!"

"The tunic you wear," Eilian explained, "will allow you to pass nearly unseen through any wooded or grassy areas. It will also protect you from heat or cold, rain or snow, and the girdle is enchanted to turn any weapon that is aimed at you."

The second item produced was a pair of golden sandals. Soft as kid leather, they buckled as high as Nikki's knees. "These will give your feet the speed you knew when I lent you my sandals," Eilian said, as she knelt to buckle the high sandals. "And they will also make you more nimble."

The last item Eilian drew out of the packages was a pair of kid gloves, golden brown and studded with silver. Nikki imagined them to have been made for some great fairy-swordswoman in days gone by. "These," Eilian said, "will enhance your swimming and climbing abilities, and will enable you to wrestle with the strength of ten men." She slipped the gloves onto Nikki's extended hands and stepped back to admire the Daughter-of-Man, about whom a golden aura shimmered as she stood in the fairy bath chamber.

"I certainly don't feel any stronger or more nimble," Nikki said, "but I can't wait to see how I look. Is there a mirror in here?"

"This way," Eilian said, motioning Nikki to follow. She led Nikki across the bath chamber to a wall hung with purple draperies. Taking hold of a silver cord, Eilian pulled it and parted the drapes to reveal a great fairy-wrought mirror of solid gold. It was a fabulous item, standing at least ten feet tall, carved with many wondrous and ancient figures. Its solid-gold surface was polished to a perfect mirror luster.

"Michael Jackson couldn't even afford this!" Nikki blurted out, as she took in the incredible sight.

"Is he the king of your land?" Eilian inquired politely.

"Not exactly," Nikki replied with a grin, as she stepped closer and looked into the mirror. A beautiful young woman, perhaps a fairy-princess, looked out of the mirror at Nikki. It took a moment for the girl to realize that it was her own reflection she was seeing. Outlined in its fairy-aura, Nikki's golden reflection suddenly juxtaposed itself in the girl's mind with the image of a vain bikini-clad Nikki Renn striking movie star poses before her bedroom mirror. Her mind raced back to that moment just before the start of this adventure. She reflected on how selfish she had been then. All she had wanted was to look as sexy as possible, to display herself as close to naked as she could for the sexual thrill of it. She had plotted it all the night before while shopping at the mall and her one intent had been to catch Paul's eye, and yes, to turn the heads of the other boys while on the beach. And she thought of Harold and how he had accused her of being naked. A slut was what he had meant. Then she remembered how Paul had admired her as she had limbered up to pose for him.

"If he could only see me now," she said to the figure of noble beauty captured in the golden mirror.

"You speak to the mirror of Paul." Eilian appeared beside Nikki in the mirror. It seemed as if the fairy had read Nikki's mind. She took one of the girl's gloved hands.

"I wanted so bad to impress Paul," Nikki said, feeling the beginning of a tear. "And Harold was right, I was just running around the neighborhood naked!"

"It is said that vanity is shed when one looks into a fairy-mirror," Eilian said. "And I have heard that vanity is one of the things which separates the Sons- and Daughters-of-Man from El Elyon."

Nikki turned away from the mirror.

"I just wanted him to like me so bad!" she cried out. "And now I don't even know if we'll ever have a life together." She heaved a sigh and continued, "One minute my biggest worry is how sexy I can be without looking like a tramp, and the next minute the whole world is gone. And I'm supposed to help bring it back! Then we're back in some might-have-been and we meet Joshua and Gwydion, and just when things are starting to go right, I find myself in a whole different world with that creepy Rae woman. When I ran away from the Rae monster, I fell into some sick cartoon world, and when I ran away from the cartoon place, a beaver," she exclaimed wildly, "led me to a door to your world!

"You are the most beautiful person I have ever known and you told me that I was beautiful when all I could see was how dirty and bruised and bleeding I was. When I look in this mirror I see myself like a princess that I don't deserve to be. I'm so confused about who I really am. Why am *I* supposed to save the world? Why me of all people? And what's happened to Paul and the others?"

Eilian reached up and wiped a tear from Nikki's eye. "The girl you see in the mirror is the one I have seen all along," the fairy said. "She is the one, like me and my people, who was created by El Elyon to live in beauty and joy. But we are all kept from the fulfillment of that joy by the evils which have befallen the multi universe, ever since the revolt of the Anointed Cherub."

"But what am I supposed to do?" Nikki asked, still bewildered.

"You are to do what you were chosen to do," Eilian returned. "And that is to save the world from the attack of Apollyon. We all serve El Elyon — The Father; and Apollyon serves the Anointed Cherub — the Anti-Father. I do not know how, but I know that Apollyon will be defeated and you will have your world back."

Nikki gathered strength from the fairy's words and pulled herself together. She turned back to her image in the mirror.

"Then I am this princess," she said to the reflection of Eilian beside her own. "With all these wonderful gifts your people have given me, I will fight like a princess and we will find a way to defeat Apollyon!"

✳ ✳ ✳

"I am Fionn," the golden-haired warrior said, as he approached Harold.

The Son-of-Man was sorting through a backpack, and he looked up at the approaching fighter. The fairy was no larger than Nikki but looked as if he could whip nine out of any ten men he came across. He wore a tunic of green gossamer with a gold breastplate. At his side he wore a long sword of fairy-make, and a shield of similar kind was slung across his back.

"I will be traveling with you to the king's palace in case you should run across any trouble," Fionn said, as he stooped to help Harold.

"Yeah." Harold pulled the straps tight on the pack and stood, hefting it to test its weight. "Trouble seems to be my middle name, lately."

The fairy-warrior's eyes widened and he stood, then bent low with a sweeping bow.

"You honor me, Son-of-Man, by entrusting me with your true name, if indeed it is," he said.

"Say what?" Harold stood up, confused by the fairy's words.

"Your true name," Fionn continued. "Everyone has a true power name. It is this which holds one's true essence, and if another knows that name it means they have power over that person. It is considered a mark of true honor and trust to allow another to know one's true name. Is this not what you meant?"

160

"Ah, yeah, I mean, no," Harold stammered, a little embarrassed. "What I mean is, well, that's just sort of my name because I seem to have found so much of it lately."

"Oh, I see!" A look of understanding took the fairy's face. "It is an event name you have chosen. Since you have seen so many troubles as of late, you deem to call yourself 'Trouble' until you have defeated them. Yes, very honorable."

The fairy bowed again.

"Please allow me to help you finish packing the pony, Trouble," Fionn said, with a big friendly smile. The fairy lifted a package to the back of the pack pony named Zebedee, which they had been given for the trip. As Fionn turned his back, Harold rolled his eyes and shook his head but had to smile at himself for letting his own joke backfire on him.

When he turned from Fionn and the pony, Harold saw Nikki and Eilian coming from the inner chambers into the great hall. A slight gold aura shimmered about Nikki, much like the auras about the fairies, due to the powerful fairy items she wore. Harold had never seen Nikki so beautiful. He stood wide-eyed and open-mouthed as the girls approached.

"Hi, kid." Nikki smiled as she came up to her brother. "You look ready for adventure! How's the packing coming?"

"Man, Nikki, do you ever look great! I've never seen you look so beautiful." Harold gasped with astonishment. Then, gathering control of his wits after seeing his sister in the radiance of her fairy attire, he added, "Zebedee here is just now packed up and ready to go."

Fionn stepped from the other side of the pony where he had just finished tightening the cinches on the baggage.

"Nikki, this is Fionn," Harold said, as the fairy-warrior stepped around the pony. "He's the one Ossian is sending as our bodyguard."

"It is the highlight honor of all my years to serve the most beautiful and honored of the Daughters-of-Man." Fionn bowed low after this pronouncement to Nikki.

The next hour was spent eating a grand meal prepared in honor of the travellers and with Fionn and Eilian receiving various instructions from Ossian, who with all the people of his sithein, gathered in the doors of the great hall to see the company off. Thus, with many "fair-ye-well's" and "God speed ye's," Nikki, Harold, Eilian, Fionn and Zebedee were off to the palace of Gwyn ap Nudd.

CHAPTER VIII

Vengeance of the Phouka

*F*or one long, uneventful day the company worked its way through the northern lands of the Tylwyth Teg. They camped the night on the western border of the lands chiefted over by Ossian, and the morning found them crossing a vast plain toward a hilly woodland.

Around midday, Fionn found what he thought to be the bootmark of an iron-shod Red Cap. Later, toward evening, they found a black arrow which convinced Fionn beyond any doubt that Red Caps had recently passed this way.

"This proves they are definitely in the area," Fionn said, turning the barbed black arrow over and over between his fingers. "They are moving lightly, to leave no more evidence of their passing than this."

"Let me see that, please." Harold reached for the arrow.

"Be careful, Trouble." Fionn handed the arrow to the boy. "It may very well be poisoned."

Harold took the arrow from the fairy and as his fingers touched its shaft, the now familiar heat flared in his fingertips. Slowly he turned, reading the rise and fall of the burning. It was not as strong as when he had been looking for Nikki, as the power of the spell was definitely growing weaker, but it was enough to give him the information he needed.

"We seem to be traveling," he said, after several moments of concentration, "in the same direction that a band of ten to fifteen Red Caps traveled around three days ago." "Fifteen?" Nikki shouted, the hand of fear gripping her stomach.

"Can your magic tell us any more, Trouble?" Fionn asked, his voice full of respect for a power he understood, and in fact, was made of.

"*Camp in safety and I will send instructions as you meditate tonight.*" The voice of Gwydion sounded within Harold's head.

"What?" Harold turned back to the fairy who'd spoken his question at the same moment the Cait Sidth's voice had touched the boy's mind.

"Harold, are you alright?" Nikki moved to the boy's side and placed a hand on his shoulder. "You seemed really spaced out for a moment there."

"Oh, yeah." The boy recovered his composure at the touch of Nikki's fairy-gloved hand. "Ah, we need to find a safe place to camp so I can do some meditation. I have some instructions coming and only by getting in mental contact with Gwydion can I receive them."

"I would suggest we make for that forest edge before camping," Fionn said, pointing to the tree line some miles to the west. "That is the border of the Andramear. She is a good forest and not infested with the forces of evil, and I doubt Red Caps or bogies of any sort have the courage to enter therein. We should be safe there."

With that they began moving again. Several hours of daylight lay ahead of them and Fionn estimated they would make the Andramear by twilight.

"After we get into the Andramear," Nikki asked, "how much longer will it be to the place of Gwyn ap Nudd?"

"It will take about one and a half days to travel through the Andramear," Eilian answered.

"I plan on two days," Fionn added. "We will make a stop at Mirrorsil to replenish our water supply."

"Ooooh," Eilian's eyes sparkled at the mention of the name. "I can hardly wait to swim again in its waters. There are great magics held within the waters of Mirrorsil, Nikki! But as you asked, once we clear the Andramear we have the rolling lands of the Mellionwear to cross and with no trouble we should make that in two days."

They pressed onward with little more talk, and just as Fionn had estimated, twilight found them entering the edges of the Andramear — a fantastic climactic deciduous forest. The wood smelled the freshest of any Nikki or Harold had ever been in. It reminded the Children-of-Man of the smell of freshly plowed land and crisp dry leaves. There was also a feel and smell to the air like that which follows after a quick spring shower, but the wood was dry, indicating no mere rain, but magic was responsible for the marvels of these woods. Harold was the only one whose footfalls made any sound in the leaves of the forest floor. The fairies' tread was so light they hardly disturbed the dust as they passed and Nikki found that her fairy-made sandals gave her much the same finesse. The land was made of low rolling hills and for an hour past twilight the company made their way through the gigantic trees. Finally Fionn motioned for them to stop.

"Here," the fairy spoke. "I think this will be our camp for the night."

The Children-of-Man could see nothing but the faint black shapes of gigantic trees about them and some lower, fatter shapes which they thought must be boulders.

"*Eclayon Esper DraShee!*" As the words rolled with echoing reverberation from Fionn's lips, pastel werelights sprung up about the woods. Blue, yellow, pink and green, the baseball-sized werelights were everywhere. They floated freely about in the air, sat on the points of branches and circled about the heads of the fairies. The entire campsite was lit with the dim pastel glow of the diaphanous puffs.

What Nikki and Harold now saw was a natural ring formation of trees and boulders which looked easy to defend and very safe.

"This is a fairy-fort," Fionn announced as the werelights danced their illumination over the scene. "Even if any evil has come into the Andramear we should be safe here. You rest, Trouble, so that you can meditate and receive instructions for us. Eilian and I will unload Zebedee and Nikki can take him to water at a brook which runs near here."

A bedroll was broken out immediately and Harold was put down for a rest. While Fionn unloaded the pony, Eilian sat by Harold and quietly sang a haunting fairy-melody which soon had the boy lost in a world of his own dreams.

"Here, Nikki my dear." Fionn turned to Nikki when the unloading of Zebedee was finished. She was watching the werelights as she sorted through things needed to make camp. Several of the pastel fuzzballs had taken up about her shoulders due to the fairy items she wore and she had begun to notice a feeling of friendliness coming from them, as if they were alive themselves.

"You can take Zebedee to water now," the fairy told her. "The brook is about a hundred yards that way."

"Come on, Zebedee old boy," Nikki called, rising from her sorting to stroke the pony's velvet nose. "We'll get you a good fresh drink of water."

She lead the pony from the light of the fairy-fort with several werelights following at her shoulders. Into the dark of the forest Nikki lead the pony with only the dim glow of the pastel fuzzballs to guide her. The girl was surprised at how much help the werelights were, for despite their dimness she did not stumble once along her way. It was as if she knew where a root or vine lay before her foot came to it. Nikki chalked it down to more fairy-magic. She thought that maybe the werelights were alive in some way. Maybe they helped her not only to see with her eyes, but also with her intuition. Whatever it was, it gave her a great deal of comfort knowing that it worked so well.

Just as they were nearing the stream Nikki heard voices. She was moving as quietly as any fairy and Zebedee, being fairy-bred, made no more noise than a squirrel, but the moment they heard the voices she and the pony froze in their tracks.

"Go get Fionn," Nikki whispered into the pony's ear. He turned and headed back toward the camp.

As Zebedee trotted quietly away, Nikki crouched in the brush and began to work her way closer to the sound of the voices. With a few moment's delicate work she was able to maneuver her way to an open spot at the side of the brook. On the other side, not ten feet from her, were three large shadowy figures having a discussion around a meager campfire.

"What we gonna do 'bout catching up with the boys, Bob?" a harsh voice rasped.

"Don't ya' be worrying 'bout that, mate," a second voice answered. "I got me plans to work around them goons."

"But Bob," came a voice from the third form. "The others ain't gonna be likin' it if we be double cuttin' 'em."

A backhanded slap from the center figure, evidently Bob, caught the third speaker in the face.

"Shut your mug, sap!" Bob growled. "If I want any opinions I'll beat 'em out of you, understand?"

The third shadow wiped an arm across his mouth.

"Well, I didn't think there was no harm in askin'," he replied.

"Why you..." The shadow of Bob's arm shot out, and he hand clenched the third form by the throat.

"Bob, wait!" The first figure suddenly rose from his crouching position.

"What you jumping for, Tom, you figure on taking me on over this?"

"Quiet!" The standing figure shot out a hand. "Take yourself a sniff around before we go to fallin' in amongst ourselves." It then made several heavy snuffles in the air.

Bob rose and began snuffling the air.

"Yeah, Tom, I see what ya' mean." Bob shot a kick at the still crouching figure. "Get off your butt and be useful, Mick, we got ferishers in the dagged woods!"

Nikki crouched low in the brush, the were-lights at her shoulders dimmed to almost nothing. Her heart pounded like a hammer and felt as if it was coming up into her throat. She prayed Fionn would arrive before the three could find her.

For several long moments it seemed they would not see her, even though their red burning eyes turned in her direction time and again. Then it all fell in.

"There, Bob," Tom shouted, then dashed right for Nikki's hiding place. "I see the dagged little gadge!"

Nikki screamed and spun to dash for safety as Tom sprang. His airborne bulk landed with a crunching thud across the very bush which, only seconds prior, had hidden Nikki. She scrambled madly up the creek bank as she heard the water torn by the mad splashing of Bob and Mick's rush to Tom's aide.

The werelights had winked out the moment Tom had sprung for Nikki so the girl struggled in the pitch black of the fairy-night.

"Don't let it get away, Tom!" Bob's voice roared over the splashing and crashing of the three in their attempt to grab Nikki.

"We'll roast it and eat it!" came the call from Mick.

Nikki's heart pounded in her ears. Her hand found the tough branch of some brush high on the creek bank and closed on it. With her feet scrambling against the steepness of the bank, she began to make some headway when the iron-like grip of Tom's hand closed about her left ankle. Her other hand joined its grip with the first on the branch, and she strained with every muscle of her body to pull from the vice grip which held her ankle.

"I got it, Bob," Tom roared as the other two came crashing up to him. "I got it, now!"

Nikki felt her left leg go out of joint as Tom gave a powerful jerk backward. Pain seared her body and the bush she grasped was uprooted as she flew backward through the air. Shadows of the black forest flew about her and disorientation pulled at the fabric of her mind.

"I got it! I got it! I got it!" Tom danced about in the middle of the creek. He held Nikki upside down by the ankle. She swung like a rag doll from the creature's huge hand. The water splashing her face from Tom's jubilant kicking and dancing about in the creek was the only thing that kept her from passing out from the pain.

"Hold what yo' got Tom, and stop all this hollering." Bob was at Tom's side now, and his hefty backhand cuffed the jubilant Tom square in the mouth.

"Hit 'im again, Bob!" Mick loped up to join his compatriots. "Hit 'im again for all his shouting!" Bob's backhand caught Mick in the mouth this time.

"I'll rip the tongues from both yer mouths iffin you keep this den up," Bob said, reaching for Nikki. "Now give me over the beast and I'll be deciding what to do with it!"

Nikki wanted to scream but the pain in her leg, and being swung about upside down kept her from doing more than making several harsh croaking sounds.

Nikki could tell little of her captors in the frenzy. They were much larger than men, though, and they were hairy and smelt like a hog pen.

"Here, Bob," Tom said, thrusting Nikki forward toward the leader. "I wouldn't want to be holding out on you, don't you know?"

Nikki saw the black shape step toward her and felt its rough, clawed paws grasp her about the waist. The world turned over as Bob pulled her from her dangling position and held her upright. His foul breath blasting into Nikki's face was enough to gag her.

"I think this one could be worth a little fun afore we go to roasting it," Bob surmised, as he looked into Nikki's face. "I'd like to see how it screams as we puts the brandin' irons to it and flays its hide!"

"You'll be unhanding the Daughter-of-Man, ye bogey beast!" The voice of Fionn boomed above the den of Nikki's captors. With it sprang to light a thousand werelights which bathed the scene in their shimmering magic. The three beasts were revealed in the light as huge gorilla-like creatures. They had arms and legs proportioned to those of man rather than ape, though, and they wore rough leather armor and red crude-knit stocking caps.

"Gods of fire and earth condemn us!" Mick cried, as he dove from the brook into the brush next to it.

"What?" Bob turned to face the fairy-warrior. He tucked Nikki under one arm. "We gets one stinking ferisher warrior to play with before we gets to put the irons to this pretty one!"

"Let me take it on, Bob." Tom was unslinging an iron-hafted double-bit axe from his belt.

"Come to me, ugly one." Fionn drew his fairy-sword and the blade burst into flame as he swung it in a ready, two-handed grip.

"I'm going for help!" Mick cried in a voice of fear as he burst from the brush.

"That's right, Mick, run away in a fight," Bob called to his fleeing companion. "Run on, you scum, I'll deal with you later!"

Mick made his mad dash for safety but before he could run twenty feet he was met full in the face by the hind feet of Zebedee. The fleeing Red Cap was knocked reeling into the creek where the faithful fairy-pony leapt upon him and began fiercely trampling him underfoot.

"It serves the slime right," Tom shouted, as Mick fell to the pony's attack. "But this one's still got you and me to contend with, eh, Bob?"

"Garn if you ain't right for once, Tom," Bob answered. He then flung the semi-conscious form of Nikki to the far bank where fortunately she landed on a pile of brush rather than upon the rocks of the bank.

"Now, let's see what this stinking little ferisher warrior is made of. A fire sword can hurt but you gots to get down two fighters of the high chief's clan. Can you do that, little ferisher?"

Bob pulled a wicked looking short black sword from his belt. Its blade was jagged with iron teeth which would yield ripping wounds if ever allowed to land a blow, and the blade was stained with some evil rust color that betrayed the presence of poison.

"Come to me, you unclean beasts," the fairy-warrior challenged. "I'll send you to serve in flames with your evil maker!"

Bob rushed the fairy, giving a blood curdling cry and with sword raised for the kill. Fionn parried the delivery of the sword and spun to catch Bob square in the stomach with a well-aimed side kick. Bob staggered back with the wind knocked out of him for the moment.

"Let me take 'im, Bob! This axe were forged for ferisher slashin'. You know how I gets when I draws it!"

Bob gave the creature a nod and Tom flew into a berserker's rage. He rushed to the attack, and his axe rose and fell with lightening speed. The blows rang from Fionn's sword as the fairy parried one after another axe-stroke. Several struck the fairy's breast plate causing blue sparks to fly. So furious was Tom's attack that it drove Fionn back up the bank and away from the reach of Bob, who had regained his breath and had begun to stride up the hill after the berserker and fairy.

Fionn's entire attention was by now riveted on the enraged attack of the rabid Tom and the battle sounds of clashing steel and cries of fury shot terror through the night. Werelights swirled and blazed as fairy fought Red Cap and slowly Fionn's strength gave way to the berserker.

At the far shore, Nikki's senses were returning. She saw the terrible battle on the other shore and tried in haste to stand. Her left leg seared her body with pain and she fell face forward into the creek. The coldness of the water dashed numbness from her mind and through the searing pain of her damaged leg she began to crawl toward the fight.

Harder and harder the berserk Red Cap fought against Fionn, and Bob taunted the fairy as he watched, sword drawn.

"Give it to him, Tom ol' boy," Bob roared in laughter, as the fairy-warrior was pressed further and further to his limit. "Any minute now he's going to give in and you'll haves his head decorating your belt!"

Nikki pulled her way across the creek and onto the bank. Tears streamed down her face as the pain from her leg burned into her consciousness. With gripping determination she pulled herself upright, balancing on her right leg. Her left, twisted and beginning to swell, dragged behind her as she hobbled her way up the side of the bank, coming ever closer to the back of the unsuspecting Bob.

"Clash him, bash him, cleave his filthy skull!"
Bob shouted, as blow after blow from the berserker's
axe fell to sword and armor of the fairy. Fionn was
barely able to lift the sword to parry now and as yet
had not delivered the first blow to Tom.

Through the den of the battle Bob was not able
to hear the hop-skip of Nikki's crippled approach
toward his rear, and by the time he felt the steel grip
of her fairy-gloves about his muscled waist it was too
late.

A croak of wild fear caught in Bob's throat as
he suddenly found himself being lifted from the
ground. He struggled to free himself from the steel-
like grip which had him, but with every twist of his
massive body, the terrible fingers dug themselves
deeper and deeper into his hide. Blood gushed
from the wounds that were being torn in his sides
by his unseen assailant, and for the first time in his
long life, the Red Cap warrior knew the true grip of
icy fear about his black heart.

"Tom, help me!" was the last cry from the Red
Cap's lips as Nikki dashed his body to the ground
with the force of ten mighty men. He landed on his
neck and shoulders and the tell-tale snap reported
the condition of his spine. The creature would never
move again.

Nikki, her gloved hands stained with blood, slowly turned her head in the direction of the fantastic battle between Fionn and the berserker Red Cap. She balanced herself with one steadying hop on her right leg, and was pushing the pain of her left leg to the recesses of her battle-conscious mind when a mighty roar split the night.

From the shadows just beyond the glow of the blazing werelights, a great black shape came through the air. It sailed with the grace of a huge jungle cat. Nikki could just make out the blur of a great black beast whose outline dazzled with fairy fire aura.

The spring of the beast carried him directly toward the berserker. Nikki watched in what seemed to be slow motion, the blazing black form floating through the air to connect with the berserker Red Cap. The beast struck the Red Cap full force in the side, driving them both into a collapsing, rolling tumble of arms, legs and weapons through the werelit underbrush. Fionn stood in shocked surprise as the leap of the black, fire-lined beast carried his enemy far away into the undergrowth. Nikki and Fionn watched as, with bellows and roars like a maddened lion, the creature rent asunder the body of what had once been Tom, the berserker Red Cap.

With sword still out and flaming, Fionn quickly moved to Nikki's side as the beast put the finishing touches to what remained of the hapless Tom. As the fairy encircled Nikki's waist with his free arm she flung her arms about his neck for support. Then the beast turned toward them.

The pain in Nikki's leg throbbed and burned but the fire in the eyes of the approaching beast kept her concentration directed toward remaining conscious. Silently the beast padded toward them. It was coal black in the glow of the werelights, with an aura that blazed fire-like about its sleek fur. It was every bit as large as a pony but looked like a cross between a dog and a cat. As it drew near, Fionn held the flaming blade out in warning as he kept a firm grip about Nikki's waist. The creature halted not ten feet from fairy and girl. The great mouth, stained with Red Cap blood, opened to reveal long white gleaming fangs.

"Greetings, friends," it said, in perfectly formed words. "I am Phadrig, warden of this portion of the Andramear. I have been tracking these killers for two days. A Phouka am I, and gladly at your service."

CHAPTER IX

Summoning at Mirrorsil

*N*ikki had passed out from her pain long before Fionn, Zebedee, and Phadrig the Phouka, got her back to the fairy-fort.

"'Tis just as well," Fionn commented gently, as he lay Nikki's limp form onto a soft pile of dry forest leaves that Eilian pulled together. "The leg must needs be popped back into joint, and that is a very painful matter."

Harold slumbered yet in an enchanted fairy-induced sleep. He had not stirred, though the noise of battle seemed to have rocked the forest to its very roots.

Eilian quickly scoured the area for several plants whose leaves she crushed, letting their juices drip into Nikki's mouth. "This will cause her to sleep with ease until shaken," she explained.

"That is good," Fionn returned. "Now, Eilian, take Zebedee and go search the camp of those Red Cap naves. Perhaps it will yield some valuable information concerning all this movement of bogies we have noticed."

Eilian gave a serious nod, and without a word, dashed from the circle of werelights with Zebedee close at her heels.

"All good folk know of the noble race of Phouka," Fionn said, turning back now to Phadrig. "But I have heard of none in this land for ages now."

"So it is," the great black fairy-beast replied. "Most of my people have crossed the Eastern Sea to the lands of King Fin Bheara. I and a few of my kinsmen have stayed to oversee some of the remaining sites of wild fairy-magic — to make sure they are not overrun by the evil bogies which now invade this land."

The great Phouka paused to slowly lick the face and shoulders of the unconscious Nikki. He then placed his two great forepaws very gently on the girl's shoulders.

"Best you pull now while her mind wanders the realm of dreams," Phadrig spoke to Fionn, after one last moist lick to Nikki's face.

With a grunt of assent, the fairy-warrior knelt at Nikki's feet and gently took her left ankle and calf in his hands. His muscled arms strained and the great paws of Phadrig pressed softly but firmly on the girl's shoulders, pulling her upper body away from Fionn's direction. For a moment they held the tension, then with a quick and deft movement of the fairy's hands, Nikki's leg yielded a resounding pop.

"Ah, now that should be the end of it." Fionn released the girl's leg. "Save for some swelling and the pain of a healing injury."

"A swim in the clear waters of Mirrorsil will heal that," Eilian spoke. She had just stepped into the circle of light having returned from the Red Cap's camp site. Fionn rose to meet her.

"What did you find?" Anticipation sparked Fionn's voice.

"This!" She dropped a bundled-up blanket to the ground and kicked it open. Within its folds were a beautiful white bow and six golden arrows, along with a sheaf of papers wrapped in a hide and tied by a leather thong.

"A fairy-bow and six golden arrows!" Fionn's voice caught with excitement.

"Arrows which never miss their mark when fired by the fairy-born," Eilian added. "These we can no doubt use on this venture."

"I trust its owner pierced many a black heart ere this prize was captured!" the Phouka spoke, as he padded silently to Fionn's side. He faced the fairy-warrior and asked, "But what about that sheaf? It contains the messages known as writing. Perhaps we have a true treasure here."

Fionn stooped and took the sheaf. He unstrung its binding, freed the bundle of papers and began to peruse them.

"These are letters from all the great chiefs of the Unseelie Court, Northern tribes of Red Caps, Brags, Bogarts, even the Fir Darrig," Fionn said, after a moment of scanning the papers. "They seek to enlist the aid of what scattered tribes we have here in the south for a great onslaught against the palace of Gwyn ap Nudd."

The fairy-warrior stood as he finished his reading, carefully placing the papers back into their protective pouch.

"We must get these to the king at once," he said to Eilian, as he re-tied the bundle. "If it were not for the need of healing for the Daughter-of-Man, I would now forgo our stop at Mirrorsil."

"If speed is of the essence, I can guide you by paths unknown to others," Phadrig put in. "With haste to break camp we can be at the Mirrorsil by midmorning. I gladly offer my services."

"Excellent!" Fionn shouted, as he clapped a hearty hand onto the Phouka's shoulder. "This will get us to the Mirrorsil and through the Andramear nearly as quickly as a straight march would have us from forest border to Mellionwear."

The fairy tucked the pouch of papers into his tunic.

"Awaken Trouble, Eilian," Fionn commanded, the urgency of their mission seizing him. "Let Nikki sleep until we be quite ready to leave out!"

Eilian awakened Harold from his fairy slumber, and following a brief introduction to the Phouka, explanations were made as to the events of the evening.

"Thus we shall have to wait on the message from your Gwydion until later," Fionn explained.

Although not very happy about putting off contact with the Cait Sidth, Harold settled into helping break camp. Within the hour everything was packed, Zebedee was loaded, and the company was ready to move out.

"We shall not wake the Daughter-of-Man," Fionn said as he gently lifted Nikki from her bed of leaves, and placed her on Zebedee's back. He followed the Phouka with Harold and Eilian close behind. The fairy-pony brought up the rear, with Nikki lying across Zebedee's packs. The nimbleness of the pony kept the slumbering girl perfectly balanced.

The way of the company was lit by dancing werelights as it moved through the massive trees of the Andramear. Phadrig led them so swiftly through brush and trees, twisting and turning on paths seen only by him, that within a few moments even Fionn, who felt he knew the paths of the Andramear well, was lost.

The company drove hard on into the wood until the strength of the fairy-gained sleep Harold had gathered began to wane. Slowly he began to fall behind the fairy-folk. At first, Eilian tried helping the boy keep up by holding to his hand in the hope it would keep him up with the Phouka's pace. Finally Harold's feet, not aided by fairy-shoes, found a root in the dimness of the path. He hit the forest floor at full gait, nearly knocking the wind out of him.

Phadrig, who had run as if in a trance and oblivious to everything but the twists and turns of his fairy-path, came to a halt. The great fairy-beast sprung around, his glowing red eyes narrowing toward Harold who was just rising to his knees and spitting dirt and leaves from his mouth. The others, halting to see what the Phouka would do, were surprised at the speed with which the beast leapt. Harold was caught in a moment of confusion and put his hands up in a defensive gesture as if he read attack in the Phouka's move. But in one deft maneuver the fairy-beast scooped the boy from the ground to his back, wheeled and dashed back to his place at the head of the company.

"Onward, brothers!" he cried as he dashed past the others. "It is my fault that we lose time. I should have realized the boy was not up to our speed when we began. Make haste and we shall arrive at the Mirrorsil even sooner than I myself reckoned."

The flight of the company lasted on through the night with Phadrig picking the intricacies of his fairy-path. Nikki slept on, with the faithful Zebedee carrying her upon his back with the care of a mother cradling her child. The great black Phouka kept Harold astride him with a deftness which compared only with the ability of Counselor when the company had ridden the time winds.

On through the wood they dashed as a rose-petalled softness lit the Elfame skies. Midmorning found them halting in a glen of such enchanted beauty that it brought tears to Harold's eyes. Ferns and flowers of every sort were lit by golden streams of sunlight beaming through the tree canopy overhead. The air was filled with the buzz and flicker of many soft and flitty things which reminded Harold of dragonflies. The far end of the glen rose in height and a tall waterfall tumbled over mossy rocks into the clearest pool the boy had ever dreamed of. The very air itself seemed filled with a strength of magic he had not felt even within the Sithein of Ossian. The entire company halted at glades edge, and in a moment of silence they drank in the beauty before them. It was Fionn who finally broke the silence.

"Behold, friend Trouble, Son-of-Man, Ellendil et Elberith, Glen of the Ancient Magic, and Llyn y Mirrorsil, the Lake of Eternal Waters!" A flourish of the fairy's hand introduced the panorama before them to Harold, who found a lump in his throat as if such beauty was more than his human form could take in without bursting into tears.

Then suddenly, as if he could wait no longer, Phadrig gave a mighty roar of delight and dashed into the glen. The Phouka kicked and bucked like a young colt as he ran. The others, as if given the proper signal, burst running and cheering into the glen. They pounced, dashed and pranced in and out amongst the growth of Ellendil. Zebedee, in spite of all his exuberance, never let the sleeping form of Nikki even slightly slip off his back.

Through butterweed and marigolds, bluebells and heather, the companions danced and ran until at last they found themselves together by the lapping waters of the magic pool, Mirrorsil. The waterfall splashed gaily on the far side, sending a dancing cascade of diamond droplets into the air. Through the droplets, sunbeams played in a rainbow chorus of shimmering colors across both rocks and pool. The sights, sounds and smells of glen and pool made Harold wonder how trouble could exist anywhere in the universe with such a magic place as this in creation. It was the voice of Fionn, however, that brought him back to the realities at hand.

"Let us get the Daughter-of-Man from Zebedee's care and wake her for a healing swim," the fairy said, standing at the boy's side.

"What?" Harold answered slowly as a person being stirred from a deep sleep, indeed from a dream which they did not wish to leave. "Oh, Nikki, yes. Eilian said these waters will heal her leg?"

"Indeed they will," the fairy-warrior said, as he moved to Zebedee's side and began to loosen the pallet they had made on the pony's back. He lowered Nikki to the lush grass which grew at the edge of Mirrorsil. "But first we must awaken her."

Eilian, her arms around Phadrig's neck and her chin resting on the beast's great black head, was already standing ankle deep in the pool's edge, as was the Phouka. "Because of the herb I gave her she must be shaken vigorously to be roused," she said. "Call her name as you shake her, Harold, for that will help to bring her back more quickly."

Harold and Fionn shook Nikki as if they were trying to awaken a sleeper in a burning house.

"Nikki? Nikki!" Harold called to his sleeping sister. "Nikki, wake up!"

Deep within a dark and dreamless place of warm peace, the mind of Nikki Renn began to remember life. Far away she heard a voice, the urgent voice of someone dear to her. The clouds of warm darkness began to part as she drifted into a semiconscious slumber, then feeling began to find its way into her mind.

"Ouch, oh..." Nikki muttered. "Something is hurting my leg, get it off," her sleepy mumble continued.

"Nikki! Nikki, wake up! It's Harold!" the boy called, as the sound of her voice caused him to shake with renewed vigor.

"Nikki, wake up!" Fionn added his call to that of Harold.

"What? Ow, my hip hurts, and my leg!" Nikki's eyes opened.

"Nikki, wake up," Harold said, looking into the girl's sleepy eyes. "Wake up, Sis, we're going to fix your leg. Fionn and Eilian have brought us to a magic pool!"

"Pool? Eilian? Oh, now I'm beginning to remember."

The girl propped herself up on an elbow. She looked around her, and the last edge of confusion wore off.

"Oh, this place is beautiful!" she exclaimed, and then added, "Eilian, what is that you are hugging?"

The fairy-girl threw her head back in laughter, reminding Nikki of the way she laughed when they had first met. She then kicked out with her foot sending a shower of magical droplets over the three.

"This is my friend, Phadrig."

"A Phouka," the fairy-beast said, turning his head to greet Nikki, "and warden of this Andramear. I don't suppose you remember our first meeting as you were in the process of blacking out."

The events of the past night, complete with a retelling of the fight, Nikki's injury and the flight through the wood were related by the company as Eilian gathered water in a great lily pad and carefully washed Nikki's injured leg and hip.

"So we have brought you here for a healing swim," Eilian said, finishing the tale. "The waters of Mirrorsil have properties which restore body, soul and spirit. Come, let us help you into the pool."

Eilian continued to pour waters over Nikki's leg to ease the pain enough so that Nikki could walk to the pool and get in. As she did so Phadrig made formal introduction of himself to the Children-of-Man.

"As warden of the enchanted wood," the Phouka said, "it is my duty to tend to the trees which come into my care."

"Then these must be more than just normal everyday trees," Harold said.

"True, young one," the Phouka replied. "The trees of Elfame are special indeed. You see, when any animal meets a violent death within the Fields of Man, its spirit comes here as a golden tree, and here it lives until it feels it is ready to go on to the work that the Great Creator El Elyon had for it. As long as the spirit lives within these fields the tree blooms and bears golden leaves, but when that spirit decides to pass on to its higher calling with El Elyon, its blooms cease and the leaves fall to the earth. It is only then that a tree of Elfame may be used for wood, for the spirit has passed on into the heavens."

"You mean that my cat Willy who was run over by a car back in Chicago is now a tree here in these woods?" Nikki asked.

"Either in my care, or that of one of my brethren," answered Phadrig.

The pain in the girl's leg was easing as they spoke, and soon she carefully rose and entered the enchanted pool. The cold waters of the Mirrorsil stirred a deep tingle within her body which began in her toes, and like icy fire shot their healing magic throughout her body. Nikki, suddenly finding herself free of pain, swam the enchanted waters, as the cold fire of their magic penetrated her every fiber. Then quickly the others joined in, and for what seemed like hours, they all laughed, splashed and played in the magical pool. All the worries of the everyday world were forgotten as the friends played and swam about.

As the company frolicked, the sun began to move behind the trees of the forest, casting bright sunbeams across the waterfall.

"Look!" Harold shouted suddenly, pointing to the top of the cascade. All playing stopped as the friends turned their attention to the waterfall.

There standing upon the topmost rock was a great golden ram, gleaming radiance in the sunshine. Fairy, human, Phouka and pony all stopped their dashing and splashing and stared in amazement at the great golden image. The fantastic creature seemed to be looking at something far away and concentrating intently, and then as if satisfied with what he saw, he turned his face down toward the swimmers. His eyes flashed red like fire, a fire that warmed the hearts of the friends in the pool but carried a hint of warning that it could just as easily burn the life from an enemy in an instant.

The ram then smiled down at the friends and the smile made the fire in his eyes burn brighter. Nikki suddenly remembered the feelings she got in the winter time when the whole family would sit by their grandfather's fireplace and feel so lucky to be members of such a loving family.

As the companions watched spellbound, the ram threw back its golden head and gave voice to a mighty lion's roar, which resounded through the forest. The glen was shaken to its very foundation by the mighty roar, and as its echoes rebounded one upon the other, the ram wheeled about and sprang into the woods. The company, in stunned silence, watched the spot where the ram had stood.

"Eben-ezer," Phadrig said, finally breaking the silence left by the last echo of the ram's roar. "The Lamb Who Became a Lion. We have heard of him but few have actually seen him. It is said he is the very son of El Elyon himself, and that he only appears when a Child-of-Man walks the lands of Elfame."

"This is a great sign to us," Fionn declared, as he turned his attention from the rock to the company. "We must be on to the place of the king. We have a mission and can play no longer."

Everyone came from the water with a freshness and renewal of spirit. Never had they felt so new.

"Somehow I feel like a completely different person," Nikki said, as she stood looking back across the pool where the ram had appeared on the water-fall. "I feel like that princess I saw myself as in your mirror back at the sithein," she said to Eilian.

"Oh, no!" Harold shouted, as they were wading from the pool. The others turned suddenly to see what was the matter.

"What is it, Trouble?" Fionn's expression had turned to concern.

"In all the excitement I completely forgot I was supposed to meditate and make contact with Gwydion. He had some kind of instructions for me!"

"Oh, boy," Nikki mused. "This could be a problem."

"You do not by any chance speak of Gwydion ab Mathonwy, High User of the Creator's deep magic, do you?" Phadrig asked.

"The very one," Harold returned.

The great fairy-beast shook himself dry then sat in a patch of soft grass near the edge of the Mirrorsil.

"I know him well," the Phouka continued, after he had sat. "And is his companion, one called Counselor?"

"That's him!" Nikki shouted, before Harold could answer. She ran quickly to the Phouka's side. "Can you help Harold get in touch with them?"

"Yeah, that would be great!" Harold exclaimed, still standing knee deep in the water.

"No. I have no way to help you make contact with Gwydion and Counselor," said Phadrig. Their enthusiasm waned a bit until he added, "The best I could do is summon them here to Elfame with us."

"Alright!" Harold shouted, as he jumped and splashed water high about him.

"I knew not you were a summoner, good Phadrig." Fionn spoke with a new respect to the Phouka. "This could very well give us the exact edge we need in our battle."

"Then let it be done," Phadrig said with resolve. "I shall call to the Fields of Elfame Gwydion the White One and Counselor the High gryphon!"

"And please," Nikki quickly added, "my boyfriend Paul is with them. He's very important to our mission too!"

"Yeah," Harold quickly put in. "We definitely need him."

Nikki shot her brother a smile. A few days ago she would have been mortified to have Harold following her about, but she had gained a whole new respect for her little brother.

"Then you should all gather behind me," Phadrig said. "All of you think on the name of El Elyon and silently call upon him for help. I shall summon the three."

All gathered behind the Phouka and sat down on the lush grass of Ellendil, and then when all were ready, the fairy-beast's voice boomed out as he began his call across the dimensions.

"*El-Elyon, Elohim; Ellendil Elley, Mirrorsil et Elberith, Cellendor Cercay. Adoni, El-Shaddiah; Atticway Anoon, Tir Nan Og en Enoway, Tuatha De Danann.*"

As the Phouka spoke the words, they felt a strange static fill the air. It was a feeling like that just prior to a great thunderstorm, and it made their hair stand on end. Suddenly at the edge of the waters of the Mirrorsil, a crinkle of energy began to flicker in the air.

For a moment, the entire company sat spell-bound in the silence which followed the booming command of Phadrig's summons. The crackle of energy picked up force and three shimmering forms began to appear within its bounds. Within seconds the shapes of three beings could be seen as transparent as glass within a crackling, pulsating cloud of pure energy. The smell of ozone filled the air like the smell of fresh rain, as one final great arc of lightning shot straight up into the air between the branches of the trees overhead. Following its resounding thunder peal, which nearly deafened the company, there stood a boy, and old man and a big white cat in the edge of the magic pool.

"Nikki, my dear, how good to see you well and unharmed," Old Joshua said, as he stepped from the ankle-deep water he had materialized in. From his attitude, one would have guessed he had been waiting at a bus stop for a ride across the dimensions and was not at all surprised at suddenly finding himself in a magic woods only seconds after being in his own study. "And Harold, I see you have found our Nikki!"

"Meruph!" Gwydion said, then began shaking the water from his paws.

"Ah, yes." Old Joshua turned his attention to the fairy-beast. "Friend Phadrig, I should have counted on your finding our friends and helping us out in a sticky situation. Now we can get down to business."

Paul had not moved, nor even budged an inch. In fact, he seemed not to have blinked an eye since his materialization. Dimension travel was still new to him and the shock from this sudden and unexpected flick from one to another had taken him somewhat aback.

Nikki quickly fixed that. "Paul!" the girl shouted, making a dash for the stunned boy. "I'm so glad to see you again!" she rejoiced exuberantly.

"Nikki!" Her touch seemed to have broken the spell. "Nikki, oh, man, have I ever been worried about you," he said, as he hugged her, then gave her a very big kiss.

"Yes, yes. This is all well and good," Old Joshua said to Nikki and Paul, as he placed a reassuring hand on the shoulder of each. "But there's much to be done yet and we have quite a lot to tell you."

At this juncture, Fionn described their journey up to the summoning, with particular emphasis placed upon the papers retrieved from the slain Red Caps, which he unsheathed and showed to Old Joshua. After this, all were in agreement that making for the place of Gwyn ap Nudd with the utmost haste was the wisest move. They gathered everything into packs, loaded Zebedee, and set out from the magical Mirrorsil, and as they traveled, Old Joshua related all he and Gwydion had discovered in their research about True Thomas, the sleeping warriors and the legend of the Sword, the Horn and the Garter. Nightfall found the company looking out over the rolling plains of the Mellionwear.

CHAPTER X

Council and Legends

*F*or the better part of two days the rolling grasslands of the Mellinowear surrounded the company as they pressed ever onward toward the palace of Gwyn ap Nudd. The only incident of the entire trip was a brief sighting of a Red Cap patrol, perhaps ten strong, which passed to the northeast of them. The members of the fellowship crouched behind a grassy knoll as Fionn watched the party of bogies pass about a thousand yards distant. Then onward they pressed, ever to the northwest, for a second day.

As they neared the end of their journey they could see a hill rising in the distance, sparkling in the sunlight. By late afternoon they lost sight of it behind a small hillock, but as they topped a rise they were met by a beautiful sight. Across the land below them stretched farms, plowed fields, and houses gathered into a village which sprawled about the foot of the tall hill they had been following. Upon this hill was the golden city of the king of the Tylwyth Teg. It gleamed gold and silver in the sunlight, and colorful banners of the clans of Elfame waved high atop its towers.

The palace stood like a crown of gold atop the city which spread from it on descending terraces reaching a third of the way down the hillside.

The hill-city was surrounded by a towered wall and moat. The only access into the city was across a great drawbridge which was itself guarded by a massive barbican. Within the wall stood the city of Elfame with shops, houses, stables and public buildings rising up the hillside in neatly contoured terraces. Wide streets and narrow alleyways laced the great city which rose to a second wall, that of the palace itself.

The palace of Gwyn ap Nudd crowned the hill with tall spires and golden towers, each sporting a banner of one of the clans of Tin Nan Og. On the south side of this second wall was the only entrance to the palace, guarded by gigantic doors of iron-banded timbers. Behind it were first the gardens and courtyards of the palace, then the stables, armories and barracks of the palace guard and finally, the grand palace itself. All this gleamed like a jewel in the sun as the fellowship stood looking across the valley from their small hillock.

A closer examination showed grim-faced fairy-warriors lining the ramparts. The great drawbridge was raised and locked. No life was seen stirring within the farming village which lay at the foot of the palace hill — void of even the normal bustle of life that should accompany a fairy-village.

"It seems the king has drawn in as if expecting a siege," Fionn said, as they stood surveying the scene from their spot atop the hillock. "I dare say they have been attacked within the past several days by roving bands of Red Caps like the ones we have seen. Gwyn ap Nudd is wise to the ways of the evil ones. Even if he is not aware of the matters we have discovered in the Red Cap packet, he will be prepared for more than just a few raiding parties."

"Let us push on to the palace moat," Old Joshua said. "We'll have to convince the soldiers atop the walls that we are not foes. From here they do not look too disposed toward friendship!"

"Meorrr uph," Gwydion grumbled.

"Yes, I suppose you may have to, my friend," Joshua returned, "but we may be able to coax our way in a little easier than that. Come on, my friends, let us be off to the drawbridge."

The company moved from the hillock and up through the plowed fields. They passed through the deserted fairy-village and began their climb up the hill on which the city stood. As they approached, the watchers upon the wall gathered toward the great main gate which was obviously the place the company was headed for. Gongs sounded inside the city and faint shouts from within drifted down the knoll. By the time the company reached the barbican, which gave egress to the drawbridge when it was down, there were a full twenty fairy-archers with notched arrows peering across the moat.

"Halt there, travellers!" called the captain of the archers from his place atop the wall. "Friend or foe, we have orders to open these gates to no one. Dire times be upon us. But if you wish, you may stay the night within the barbican. However you must be on your way upon the morrow, good folk."

"Most kindly spoken, my dear captain," Joshua called his answer up to the soldier, "but it is concerning these dire times that we travel here to speak with the good king Gwyn ap Nudd."

"My friend," the captain shouted, "message or not, friend or foe, my orders are to allow no one entrance herein!"

"Merrriff!" Gwydion suddenly growled and spat, bucking and prancing his way to the front of the company.

"MERRR-OWWWREOOWWW!" The Cait Sidth called up the wall and back to the company. Then a bolt of energy shot from the cat straight up into the air. Joshua held out an arm to move Nikki, Harold and Paul back from their nearness to Gwydion. The warriors upon the wall drew taut their bows in anticipation of an attack, but no attack came. Instead, the cat began to grow. Another bolt of lighting flashed toward the sky and the cat, now panther size, reared onto hind legs and an amazing transformation began to occur.

Gwydion's form began to shimmer and shift, like an image in a pool when the surface of the water is disturbed. He flashed, shimmered and crackled with energy and then a mighty whirlwind burst around his form. Every evidence of the form of a cat vanished, and there in the Cait Sidth's place stood a tall, grim, lean-faced man robed all in white with arms raised above his head. In his right hand he held a staff which sprouted and bore a large and beautiful almond. For some reason, Nikki's mind raced back to the old science films she had watched so many times in school, the ones which showed flowers sprout and grow in time-lapsed photography. The staff first shot forth a bud which quickly grew into a shoot. It next produced a bud which blossomed and formed into an almond in only seconds. This most definitely got the attention of those on the wall.

The captain gave a gasp heard by all below, then he ordered his archers at ease.

"I am Gwydion ab Mathonwy, holder of the deep magic of the Creator, wielder of the Staff of Aaron and Robe of Elijah!" The old man's voice boomed up the palace walls like thunder. "Now stop all this playing orders and let down the drawbridge, you ninnies!"

"At once, my lord!" the captain shouted. "Hail bridgeman, lower the drawbridge, at once. Gwydion has returned!"

"Well, I'm impressed," Harold said, as the drawbridge creaked and rumbled downward.

Gwydion turned his lean old face toward the boy.

"We would have been here the live long day bantying words with these silly soldiers if I had not done something." He reached out and grabbed Harold by the arm, pulling the boy to his side. "Come along, Harold, my boy. Don't just stand there with your face hanging out like you've seen a miracle or something! Get up."

The drawbridge landed at their feet with a thud as Harold was just getting himself adjusted to what he thought an apprentice should look like. Gwydion cast a glance over his shoulder at Nikki and Paul.

"You two try to keep your eyes and ears on business and not on each other for now," he said, while a sly grin creased his old face. He then turned back to face the open gate before them, clasped one hand on Harold's shoulder and placed the other on the back of Joshua. "Now, let us enter and see what lies before us."

A great reception awaited the fellowship as they entered the city. Folk poured from every doorway to catch a glimpse of the visitors. A whispered message passed from person to person, that "Gwydion has returned; the White One is back!"

The streets looked to Nikki as if they were truly paved with gold. Every building was ornately carved, painted and decorated with such intricate detail that the Children-of-Man were nearly awestruck by their beauty. Brightly colored pixies flitted about doors and around windows. Werelights could be seen resting about every point and high place in the homes and shops.

"Hail, Gwydion of the White!" A new fairy-captain entered from an iron door which led from barracks housed within the side of the city wall. "How long has it been since I laid eyes upon you, old friend?" The warrior approached, and Gwydion halted to meet him.

"Olwen, you old war horse, you know how very long it has been?" Gwydion grasped the friendly hand offered by the fairy-warrior as they came together. "Well met in this dire hour my dear friend, and how is Gofannon?"

"Your brother still forges the best metals in the whole of Elfame," Olwen returned. "I only wish he were here now to craft new blades for our soldiers in this dark hour. However, his journeys are nearly as tiresomely long and winding as yours. He is presently upon the shores of Tirfo Thuinn by invitation of King Fin Bheara. But let me not hold you up here. I will escort you and your company directly to the king, for no doubt you bear news of what brings these raids of dark ones from the north upon us."

With that the company was escorted through the streets of the great city and through the gate of the palace grounds, into the royal dwelling itself. The Children-of-Man were amazed at what they saw upon entering the fairy-palace. The entire building was carved of the finest woods and stones. Rich carvings covered every wall, even the ceilings. Fine statues lined the halls which were draped with arms and armor, and fine tapestries. Through a wonderland of architecture and design the company was led until at last they arrived at the massive doors to the great hall of King Gwyn ap Nudd.

The great doors were swung open for them and they passed beneath what Nikki later remembered as the most ornately carved archway she had ever seen. Into the great hall itself they came and stopped. Around them milled the highest lords and ladies of Elfame and at the far end, seated on a golden throne on a raised dias, was King Gwyn ap Nudd, upon whom they all attended.

At this point Gwydion took over the lead. Politely he moved to the front of the company, a hand still planted firmly on Harold's shoulder. He strode purposefully forward toward the throne. All eyes turned to watch their advance.

"Three things to remember, my boy," Gwydion spoke to Harold as they marched toward the throne. "One, keep your mouth closed unless asked a direct question. Two, always agree with anything I say whether you know what I'm talking about or not, and three, oh, well, if ever in doubt, refer to number two." The last point was made with another of his wry grins and a twinkle in his dark eyes.

They approached the dias, where formal introductions were made all around. Of course, the king had long known Gwydion and Old Joshua. He knew of Ossian and welcomed Fionn and Eilian as brother and sister to his court. He spoke very politely to Phadrig, sending his best wishes to the wardens of the enchanted woods. However, his special interest was turned to the three Children-of-Man, and to the packet which had been recovered from the Red Caps.

Gwydion and Joshua attempted to give a cursory coverage of the entire adventure, but it was soon evident that more time than an audience at the throne was going to be needed for this matter. So the king ordered the great hall cleared of all save his top advisors, and an emergency meeting of the great council was called.

Here Nikki, Paul and Harold told their stories in great detail, going far into the fairy-night with all the questioning and debate which followed. Several times they were called upon to retell an important portion over and over again so that the council could ponder and discuss the deepest meanings of each event. Great tomes which went back to ancient times were brought out and all the stories of old wars were pulled out. Lastly, the story of True Thomas was related every which way to the quest before them.

It was finally decided that Joshua and Gwydion were indeed correct in their determination that the Sleeping Warriors were somehow the answer to squelch the threat to all good folk from the minions of the Evil One. At length, it was determined that the company should set off as soon as possible for the cottage of Thomas and the mound where the warriors slept.

As the fairy-night grew very late, the king dismissed everyone except for Nikki, Paul, Harold, Old Joshua and Gwydion.

"I have kept you back for a reason," the king began, as the hall was cleared and the five sat back down at the table with the king. "But the hour is late so first let me call for some refreshments for the Children-of-Man."

With a clap of his hands servers, were summoned and all were served with ice-cold birch beer and walnut-oat cakes.

"Now that we are somewhat refreshed," the king said, as the company continued sipping cold draughts of birch beer, "I wish to relate to you something which may, I feel, have an important bearing upon the outcome of your mission. It is the matter of your vision of Eben-ezer at the pool of Mirrorsil."

Everything the king told the company cannot be repeated herein but he explained how the very oldest stories of Elfame related the appearance of Eben-ezer to great happenings within the kingdom of the Creator.

"The stories," the king said, "tell of how Eben-ezer is the very son of the Creator, El Elyon Himself. They also tell of a great mystery — that Eben-ezer came into the Fields of Man, born as a lamb only to die and be reborn as a lion. This event is spoken of by the ancient sages within the Fields of Man as the coming of Meshiach ben Yosef and Meshiach ben David." Here the king paused a moment as if in deep thought.

"This is a matter we cannot fully understand and I have been told that even the mighty Archangel Michael finds it a mystery — those things wrought

in the Fields of Man by Eben-ezer. It is something
of great curiosity that he and his Elohim would
desire to look into." The king paused again to take
a deep drink of birch beer.

"I do not know what it is," the king finally said,
"but I feel there is something of this story that will
be of help to you as you near the end of your quest."

At length, the discussions and ponderings came
to an end, and Nikki, Paul and Harold were shown
to their quarters where they were offered hot scented
baths and soft beds of silk and down. They slipped
into the deep and refreshing sleep of Elfame almost
before their heads hit their pillows.

It was early morning when Nikki began to rouse
from sleep. She thought she heard the sound of
distant thunder, but as sleep cleared from her mind
it became clear that what she was hearing were
massive gongs somewhere deep within the palace.

Within moments, Eilian burst into Nikki's quarters. "Nikki, get up quickly!" The fairy-girl spoke
hurriedly. "A dark army of bogies has been sighted
not a day's march north of the palace. The king calls
for us at once!"

Renewed from the night's sleep, Nikki leapt up
and dressed. Within moments, the two were in the
hallway where they were joined by Fionn with Paul
and Harold. Guards and attendants rushed to and

fro in the hallways as the five made their way to the great hall of the king. By the time they arrived there, Gwydion and Old Joshua were already in council with the king, studying over a parchment map spread before them on a great oak table.

"Oh good, the Children are here," Gwydion said, looking up from his study of the map.

"Nikki, Paul, Harold." Old Joshua spoke to the three without looking up from his concentration on the map. "We seem to have awakened with a bit of a problem. Come and take a look at this."

The three, along with their two fairy-friends, moved closer to the table where they could get a good look at the large map.

"Now, where were those blasted bogies spotted, old son?" Gwydion queried the king as all now looked down at a relief map of the land of Tir Non Og.

"Right here," the king said, stabbing a finger at a range of mountains north of the palace. "And here we are," he further indicated.

"How does this fit into our situation?" Nikki asked, as she strained to see where the king was pointing.

"Well, one of my companies of advanced scouts located a very large army of Red Caps, bogarts and other bogies right there," the king put in. "The scouts arrived early this morning with their report that the army is no more than a day to a day-and-a-half march away."

"I'd say it looks as if you are in for a real fight of it," Gwydion commented. "And if we are caught within the palace walls when the attack begins we could be sieged up here for a blasted long time."

"Yes," Old Joshua concurred. "We are going to have to leave at once if we expect our quest to have any chance of success."

"And if you do not succeed," the king added grimly, "I fear what fate awaits our fair land."

"This is the work of Apollyon," Nikki stated flatly. "I just know it is. He must have located us here and is making another try at destroying us so we can't bring back into creation our universe of the Fields of Man."

"I believe you are quite right, my dear," Old Joshua answered Nikki's comment. "The sooner we are off to locate True Thomas, the better."

"I will see to it that you are equipped with food and weapons," the king put in. "But I fear I will be able to spare no soldiers for your quest. I will need every available fairy on the walls when this attack falls."

"Oh, quite so," Gwydion interjected. "And I don't suppose you should be sending a mass of clubfooted soldiers anyway. They would do nothing but slow us down, possibly hindering us at every possible turn. We'll be off with what supplies you can provide, and nothing else to slow us down."

"But Your Majesty's kind thought is most graciously offered," Old Joshua was quick to add. "I fear my dear friend here is a bit gruff at times, where even in the form of the noble Cait Sidth he is hard-pressed for manners."

"It is no time to bandy nice words and pretty phrases," Gwydion grumbled mildly. "We have worlds to save, and no time for hurt feelings."

"Be that as it may," the king said, with a kind smile, "I take no offense at noble Gwydion's words. He speaks truth when he talks of need for hurry, so let us be about it!"

With that the company was shown to a readying room in the palace. They were all outfitted for the journey. Fionn was given a new sword, one of much higher quality than the one he had brought with him from his home. Eilian was given additional arrows to go with the arrows she had recovered from the Red Caps, and Zebedee was lightly loaded with supplies, since speed was a major consideration. Paul was placed in charge of Fionn's old sword and given several fast lessons on how to hold and swing it in a manner that would do the most damage to an enemy and the least to himself. Nikki, dressed in the gifts given her by Ossian, and Paul and Harold were each given fairy-sandals that would speed their feet and silence their movements.

Gwydion had excused himself until the party was nearly finished equipping itself, then he returned.

"Harold my boy, I have a gift for you," the old man declared, as he strode up to the party. He held out a smith's hammer, which Harold accepted. The boy then gave a questioning look up at his mentor.

"It is the hammer given long ago into the trust of my brother, Gofannon," Gwydion explained. "It is the hammer of Saint Dunstan. It will not only forge the finest metals, but will also deal a blow to any evil creature that you would not believe! I now charge you with its keeping for the duration of this quest."

Harold hefted the hammer in his hands. A thousand questions were in his mind, but from the look in Gwydion's dark eyes he knew they would have to wait for another time.

Phadrig came in from a run about the countryside he had made shortly after the return of the scouting party. He told the company what he had seen firsthand and concurred with the king, Old Joshua and Gwydion that to be back on the road with their quest was the best move.

As the fellowship moved toward the courtyard of the palace they were greeted and encouraged by many fairy well wishers within the halls of the king. Soldiers, lords, courtiers and servants all had blessings and words of strength for the eight travelers as they crossed the hallways and moved into the courtyard of the golden palace.

Once the party reached the courtyard, the king himself came out onto the balcony of his audience chambers and addressed the people who had gathered below to see off the group of adventurers. The king spoke to his people about the army of the north which was advancing upon them, and of the coming siege of the city. He told of the death of the Fields of Man by the hand of Apollyon, and of the goal of the fellowship's quest. Then, in the old high tongue of Fairy he lifted a mighty petition to El Elyon and blessed the fellowship in the name of Eben-ezer.

Once again the companions traveled through the majestic gates of the palace of Gwyn ap Nudd. They crossed the drawbridge to the cheers of the assembled fairy-folk within the courtyard and the soldiers upon the walls. Through the barbican they passed and then moved down the road through the deserted fairy-village. From there they turned to the northeast, in the direction of the cottage of True Thomas. As they passed from the village and rounded the far end of a small expanse of woods, Nikki could still see the palace of Gwyn ap Nudd gleaming golden upon the fairy-hill. She wondered what terrors the dark army would bring with its siege and if she would ever again see those beautiful halls in all their splendor.

CHAPTER XI

The Battle of Table Rock

I suppose you guys know where we're going," Harold said, as the fellowship moved on.

"Of course we do, my boy, don't be silly!" Gwydion crabbed. "We wouldn't start out on a mission as important as this, hog wild and pig crazy!" "Before you came into the great hall this morning," Old Joshua spoke up, "we had discussed the matter in some length with the king."

"We are to travel in this direction," Gwydion said, indicating the northeast path they were taking. "Around midday we will come to a place called Table Rock."

"That is a great upthrust of rock about the size you know as a football field," Joshua added. "We will then push onward."

"By evening," Gwydion again put in, "we should find ourselves by the river Cellerdore and at the cottage of a silly gnome named Tom Tit Tot."

"Old Tom is far from silly, my friend," Old Joshua quickly corrected his crotchety companion. "In fact, he is very loyal to the king and will ferry us downriver on his boat to a place known as the Cabbage Patches. It is there we are to find the cottage of Thomas the Rhymer."

For the rest of the morning the fellowship pushed onward in virtual silence. Harold, Gwydion and Old Joshua led the way, with Nikki and Paul behind them. Eilian led Zebedee close after them, and Fionn with Phadrig took up the rear.

About an hour before noon Phadrig stopped dead in his tracks. His ears perked up and his whiskered snout sniffed the air.

"What is it, old friend?" Fionn stopped by the fairy-beast's side.

"Hold up here for a moment," Phadrig said to the company, which had not all come to a complete stop. With that the Phouka dashed northward with a spurt of blinding speed. He shot like a black flash over a small rise a few hundred yards north of where the fellowship waited, and then disappeared.

"What do you suppose got into him?" Paul queried.

Nikki slipped her hand into Paul's, almost unconsciously. "From what I know of him he must smell or hear something he thinks is a danger," Nikki said.

For about five minutes the fellowship waited on Phadrig's return, and then he suddenly reappeared over the same rise where he had disappeared. He dashed up to them.

"Quickly," he panted. "There is little time. A band of Red Caps is moving in this direction. They are about one league north of us and must have picked up our scent, for they are coming right for us!"

"How many are there?" Fionn asked.

"I counted about twenty or twenty-five," the Phouka returned. "And they are armed as a war party!"

"To Table Rock!" Fionn shouted.

"That's a very good idea," Old Joshua concurred. "That is, if we can manage to get there first."

"Well, for crying in the rain barrel, let's get a move on it and stop trying to impress each other with our fancy plans!" Gwydion snapped.

"Now I understand why he was such a grumpy cat," Nikki said in an aside to Paul, as they broke into a run.

The company ran for the next forty-five minutes at a speed that would have long left the Children-of-Man exhausted and far behind had it not been for the fairy-sandals they wore. Phadrig led the way with Fionn covering the rear. Eilian still led Zebedee who ran with a swiftness close to that of the Phouka. Nikki and Paul ran hand-in-hand and for "old men" Gwydion and Joshua held their own very well, just in front of Fionn.

"If I were still the Cait Sidth I could save myself all this trouble by riding that silly jackass!" Gwydion groused, meaning he could ride on the back of Zebedee. The pony made a nickering sound at being called a jackass. Gwydion's only response was, "Well, that's your opinion, Donkey!"

"I see it!" Eilian shouted as Table Rock appeared before them.

"And I see them!" Fionn shouted back, as a band of twenty-five raving Red Caps broke the rise about five hundred yards north of them.

The sight of the enemy so close at hand brought a renewal of effort from each of the company as they strained every fiber in their beings to reach the massive range of rock before the enemy.

Nikki saw it rising before them, a huge expanse of solid stone more than fifty yards across and twice as long. It stood about three feet higher than the surrounding land and was bordered by a naturally formed crenulation of lumps and bumps, as if it were designed as a fortress. Here and there were ramp-like extensions of rock which led from ground level up to the surface of Table Rock. The top of the formation was anything but smooth, however. Its surface dipped and rose, forming troughs, gullies and ridges.

The company hit the closest "ramp" a hundred yards ahead of the charging Red Caps, who were now unleashing blood-curdling war cries and brandishing great swords of cold black steel.

"Spread out! Take the battlements!" Fionn shouted orders as everyone scurried for a defensive position.

"There are too many rampways up here!" Paul shouted back, his sword flashing sunlight in his hands. "We need to draw back and circle up!"

"Yes, let the wretches come up!" shouted Gwydion. "We'll give them something to remember us by!"

Phadrig leapt to a high ridge of rock. "Counselor, we are in need of you!" he shouted to Old Joshua.

"I do believe you are right, my friend," the old man returned, as the air about him began to shimmer and crackle with energy. Within the wink of an eye there stood the mighty form of Counselor. The gryphon reared upon his hind legs and lashed his great maned head.

"Alright! I have a great idea!" Harold suddenly shouted, as the Red Caps neared a rampway and began their way up to the top. The boy turned and ran to Zebedee where he quickly rummaged through the baggage.

"What are you doing, Trouble? It is time to stand and fight!" Fionn called out.

"I've got something important here that we can use!" Harold shouted back, just as Fionn turned to strike a blow at a Red Cap who had just reached the top of the rock. The Red Cap parried the blow but

was booted from his position on the rock by a swift kick which Fionn used to back up his sword swing.

"I've got it!" Harold exclaimed, as he drew his skateboard from a pack. "Now let them come up here, we'll just see how they can handle 'The Executioner!'

Red Caps poured over the natural ramparts of the rock as Harold hit his skateboard. He kicked off and sailed down a sharp dip and up the other side. High into the air he flew where he executed a full turn-about as he withdrew the *Hammer of Saint Dunstan*.

Nikki delivered a haymaker punch to the stomach of an advancing Red Cap with her fairy-gloved fist. The monster doubled over, just as Harold raced back down the dip and up the other side. He broke the lip of the depression, again going airborne, and swung the hammer at the doubled-over Red Cap beside his sister. The hammer landed solidly on the iron helm of the monster. Blue fire flashed as the helm split along with the skull of the evil creature, who fell backward with a jerking response of nerve reactions.

"Don't be a show-off," Gwydion called from his position upon the "battlements" of the rock.

"Solid blow!" Fionn shouted to Harold, and he then turned quickly to another Red Cap who was swinging on him with a huge two-handed sword. The fairy-warrior parried the blow and spun full circle, delivering a blow which caught the enemy across his iron-studded leather kidney belt. The blow cut part way through the armor, bringing a bellow of pain from the monster. It turned to swing again and Paul delivered a forward thrust which caught the beast in the solar plexus as it turned. The creature's momentum was so great that it ripped a gash in its own abdomen and pulled the sword from Paul's grip.

The creature sank to its knees as Paul's sword fell to the rock. Fionn stepped forward and be-headed the beast with a powerful swing of his new sword.

"Your blade, Paul!" Fionn shouted as another Red Cap raced to engage them.

Paul dove for the sword. He landed belly first before it, just as the iron-shod foot of a Red Cap clamped down on the weapon. The beast bellowed some victory shout in its crude language as it stood with sword poised above Paul. Paul closed his eyes and muttered, "Goodbye Nikki," as the sword descended. But the cry which rent the air was not Paul's. He looked up in surprise to see the Red Cap standing above him, sword held in mid-swing, with a golden arrow lodged through his throat. The beast tottered for a moment before falling backward with a loud crashing of armor.

Counselor leapt into the midst of the charging Red Caps and mighty bellows and roars were rising from the group. Several bogies flew into the air, rent asunder, and the others were trying with all their might to disengage the terror which had a death grip on them.

Phadrig had in his mouth one Red Cap by the nape of the evil creature's neck. He dragged it along, as his mighty forepaws struck two others down with ripping blows to their midsections.

Harold was airborne again, speeding to the lip of another bowl-shaped section of the rock. As he landed, he engaged two more of the enemy. One swung at him with a sword as he sped by, missing by mere inches. The second took a blow from the hammer directly to the chest. As blue fire spurted from the hammer, the iron breast plate split apart. The creature's upper armor fell off, revealing a crushed rib cage oozing black blood. The Red Cap fell to his knees gasping and coughing foul blackness from his mouth. His companion turned to get another swing at Harold as the boy fell back onto the rear wheels of his skateboard, lifted the nose into the air, and spun.

As Harold pushed off, the creature charged with sword raised for a blow. The boy shot toward the beast but before he could get to his target, the Red Cap suddenly drew up short, stopped still in its tracks; a look of shock and surprise in his dying eyes. Then slowly he fell forward, before Harold, landing on his face with a thud, a golden arrow sticking from his back.

A mass of Red Caps who no doubt felt that discretion was the better part of valor, broke from the fray and fled from the rock.

Gwydion, who had stood his ground upon one of the rampart rocks, had bashed several of the advancing Red Caps back to the ground with the deft use of his staff. Every time a Red Cap came near the old man, the beast found himself with fewer teeth in his mouth than before. The old man now spied the fleeing beasts.

"Oh, no you don't, you ugly sons-of-wretches!" the old man shouted in the direction of the terrified Red Caps. "You're not getting off that easy. You baboon-faces wanted a fight and that's just what you are getting!" With that, Gwydion raised his staff high above his head and called in a loud voice. "*El-Elyon ellion adonothia!*"

The heavens split as flashes of blue fire fell into the midst of the fleeing Red Caps. Thunder pealed deafeningly, the impact striking the rock and earth with a concussion which nearly bowled everyone off their feet. The running bogies flew high into the air and landed in piecemeal fashion about the hills.

As the thunder cleared, Harold popped to the top of a ridge, bounced from his skateboard and kicked it into his hands. He surveyed the surrounding area. Dead Red Caps lay crushed and bleeding all about them. Paul and Fionn circled back to back, swords outstretched, seeking any enemy left. Nikki held a struggling Red Cap in a sleeper hold as it kicked out its last struggle before choking to death. One last fleeing beast fell with a golden arrow in its back as Eilian quickly drew and notched another, turning to seek another target. Counselor was on the ground before the Table Rock. He had a struggling Red Cap in his jaws and shook it like a rag doll until it soon struggled no more. Phadrig sat amongst several bodies of the enemy and was bathing his face with a great forepaw, the way a cat washes.

Zebedee looked out from behind a rise where he had been hiding and nickered.

Gwydion walked over to where Harold was standing with skateboard in hand. The boy hefted the hammer in the other. The old man clapped a hand on the boy's shoulder and smiled broadly.

"Well, I suppose you can be a show-off now and then," he said with the familiar twinkle in his dark eyes. "Now, I suppose we had better take stock of our situation."

As the fellowship gathered to inspect their wounds, they were surprised to find so little harm had occurred to them. Nikki had a large bruise and abrasion on her left thigh where a hobnailed foot had kicked her. Paul had a torn tank top and skinned-up stomach from his dive to the rock. Fionn sported several minor sword cuts and one large gash in his armor just over his heart. Phadrig and Counselor were covered with scratches and small cuts. Eilian, Gwydion and Zebedee were the only ones to come out unscathed.

Fatigue took its toll, though, as the party settled down from the fight. Once the adrenaline rush was ended, everyone found that the one thing most desired was a meal and a good rest. They moved to the far end of the rock to be away from the dead Red Caps. Zebedee was unloaded and food stuffs were taken out for the midday meal. They lunched on fresh baked cakes of various nut flavors and dried fruit. Eilian brewed a nice pot of birch tea for them and passed out fresh honeycomb for desert. Following the meal they all rested. Everyone lazed about the rock as insects buzzed the air. In the distance a loon was heard faintly calling. Gwydion said it would be in the Morrodown Marsh about two leagues north of them. All in all it felt like many a lazy late-summer day which Nikki had known.

The girl sat in a shady depression of the rock with Paul, who dozed with his head in her lap. Harold pulled a Swiss army knife from his pocket. With the tool attachments he was removing the wheels from his skateboard. He oiled them with lamp oil from Zebedee's packs, then replaced and adjusted them to his satisfaction.

Fionn sharpened swords with a whetstone he'd carried in a small pouch at his side. Counselor, now Old Joshua again, rubbed oil into several of the larger cuts which Phadrig had suffered, and then tended his own, which were minor. Gwydion sat in a very sunny spot on the rock, and although occasionally he grumbled a complaint about time being wasted, he never seemed disposed to get up and start the party moving.

After an hour had passed since their meal, Old Joshua finally rose and turned to Gwydion.

"Alright, for goodness sake," he addressed his old friend. "Stop your grumbling. Let's all get up and be on our way! We will just be able to make Old Tom's cabin by dusk."

"It's about bloody time!" Gwydion responded. "I thought we were all going to turn into statues, we've stayed on this rock for so long. We have a mission before us. Let's get a move on." He looked to Harold, who sat spinning the wheels of his skateboard. "And will you please place that confounded contraption back in the bag? I've never seen the likes of the gadgets young folks come up with these days!" he muttered, as he stalked past the boy to take the lead of the march.

Harold chuckled to himself as he replaced his skateboard on Zebedee's back. He was really beginning to love this crotchety old wizard with his funny ways and his powerful life in the service of El Elyon.

With everyone roused from the afternoon's rest, the fellowship started off for the cottage of Tom Tit Tot.

CHAPTER XII

True Thomas

*T*he company encountered no further evidence of the enemy for the rest of the day, and evening found them nearing the friendly lights of a small cottage. It sat nestled beneath several huge chestnut trees on the bank of a beautiful blue river. The smell of roasting chestnuts and freshly baked bread drifted out on the evening breeze.

As they neared the cottage, they heard the music of a fiddle start up within. In the yard, three goats were just finishing their evening grazing and a dozen chickens were looking about for their nest for the night. A small golden-colored rat terrier barked and left its place on the porch, running to meet the party. With the bark of the dog, the music from within stopped as suddenly as it had begun. The dog stopped at a gate which stood open in a hedge fence which surrounded the cottage. He barked in a friendly manner and wagged his tail as the front door of the cottage opened and a man about as tall as Harold appeared, silhouetted by the light from within.

"Who stirs about the night?" a high-pitched voice called from the doorway. "Be ye friend or foe?"

"I am Gwydion ab Mathonwy," Gwydion called out, "on business of His Majesty, Gwyn ap Nudd."

"There be more than one of ye there!" the shrill voice answered. "If indeed ye be who ye say, then tell me, what be the color of Mr. Whiskers?"

"The Cait Sidth appears as white as the robe I wear," Gwydion called back. "Now, if you're finished playing guessing games with us, we are all bloody tired and bloody hungry from fighting Red Caps on our way."

The small figure turned from the door for a moment, and when it turned back it held a blazing lantern.

"I'll just be stepping out to the gate to meet ye before I be letting you into my home this night, if ye don't mind so much."

With that the silhouetted figure moved from the doorway to the porch. Down the steps it came and across the yard to stand before Gwydion and the company at the gate. Nikki could make out the shape of a little man dressed in earth tones and sporting a long brown beard.

The lantern light played about the faces of the company, illuminating them one by one. When it finally lit the faces of Nikki, Paul, and Harold, the little man gasped and stepped back. "By the horns of the Billy Goat Gruff, there be Children-of-Man in the fields!" he shrieked.

"Friend Tom," Old Joshua began, while the little man stared in wonder at the three. "We have come a full day's march from the palace, and as my companion has said, have fought a band of Red Caps along the way. We are on a dire mission which will seal the fate of all good folk. Even as we speak, a dark army from the north surrounds the palace of Gwyn ap Nudd. May we come in and tell you our story over a mug of cold brew and some fresh bread?"

"Children-of-Man in the fields of Elfame!" the little man muttered again. "Yes, yes indeed! Do come inside." He waved the company through the gate. "Forgive me my distrust, but strange things have been passing the world these few weeks. Of course come in, all of you come in. Come, Tippy!" The little man turned from addressing the company and spoke to his small golden dog who obediently turned and daintily pranced alongside his master as he lead the company back to the homey lights of the cottage.

"Nonnie, set some bowls out!" the gnome shouted, as he stomped up the wooden steps and onto the porch. "Gentry be a'callin' and they bring Children-of-Man! Set out eight, there be a flock of 'em and one be a Phouka!"

The gnome and his little dog Tippy lead the party into the cottage. It was a warm and cozy cottage with a big fire going in the stone fireplace and a big wooden table set with ten chairs about it. Nikki's mind flashed back to her first meeting with Eilian.

The woman, who now busied herself about the kitchen fetching bowls from cupboards and spoons from drawers, was as beautiful to her as Eilian had been on that first meeting.

"She's a dryad!" Eilian undertoned into Nikki's ear, having noted the look of wonder on Nikki's face as she watched the tall blonde woman work about the kitchen.

"That is true, my dear." The woman smiled, obviously overhearing the whisper across the room and above the clatter of the company finding seats at the table. "I am the keeper of these, the last of the chestnut trees, which surround our home. I am called Nonnie, and you have already met my little husband Tom. We're very happy to have you with us this evening."

She carried the bowls and spoons to the table where she set out eight places. Next to the fireplace, Phadrig's place was set out, a nice large bowl on a fine mat of woven straw.

Nonnie was dressed in a simple sleeveless gown of white which reached to the ankles of her bare feet. It was spun of cotton and trimmed with a border of embroidered green leaves which perfectly complimented the fine lines and fluid movements of the woman who now busied herself dishing porridge into the bowls she had just set.

Over a nice hot meal, acquaintances were made and the story of the fellowship's quest was told.

"I know well the Cabbage Patches," Tom told them. "Anyone crossing them will come next to a magical bean field and those who wander therein get lost, only to turn up down river days later with no memory of where they have been. It is said an old hermit lives beyond them and that he has *magicked* the bean field to keep unwanted travelers out. I believe that would be the True Thomas you speak of."

Joshua and Gwydion agreed with Tom's thought, and after some further discussion and plans for the boat trip down river on the morrow, it was decided that an early evening would be best for all. After Nikki, Paul and Harold had moved the table, chairs and several other items of furniture out of the center of the room, Nonnie and Tom set out soft pallets for all the travelers. Tom and Nonnie climbed a ladder into an attic room where a great four-post bed awaited them, and the others settled about the room on their pallets. Sleep came quickly to the weary travelers.

Nikki soon found herself in a dream world forest much like that of the Andramear. She wandered beneath the great golden trees of the forest with the fresh smell of the Elfame world around her. Soon she came to a crystal brook which she began to follow, enjoying its beauty and listening to its babble mingling with the soft rustle of the great trees overhead. In a moment, she stopped and knelt beside the brook. There she scooped up a handful of the cold clear water and put it to her mouth. As she drank of its freshness she suddenly became aware that she was being watched. With a start, she looked up and just across the tiny brook opposite her stood the great golden ram, Eben-ezer.

"Nikki my child, do not be afraid," the magnificent creature said, in a powerful but soft and well-modulated voice. "You are dreaming and it is here that I have chosen to appear to you."

Nikki stood carefully. She was not afraid of the great ram, but there was a power and majesty about him that lent a great respect to her attitude.

"I am not afraid of you, sir. I don't know why. I feel that I should be, but you seem to be so kind that I don't have fear," she said to the golden ram.

"You gave your heart to me when you were but a child because you had heard the tales of my coming into the Fields of Man, and that is how you know me. Your spirit recognizes me even in this world."

"Who are you, Great Ram?" Nikki asked, and took a step into the brook toward the great creature.

"I am the son of El Elyon. I am the Afikomen, the 'Coming One,'" the ram replied, "and this is the form in which I appear to my subjects within the Fields of Elfame. You know me by another name within the Fields of Man."

"This El Elyon that you say is your Father," Nikki began, "I have heard my friends speak of him. Who is he?"

"I and my Father are one," the Ram continued. "To know me is to know my Father, and you, dear Nikki, are a child of my heart. Come closer, child."

Nikki crossed the brook and stood next to the great ram. His golden wool smelled of fresh woods and as she came up to him, Eben-ezer breathed on Nikki. His breath was as fresh as a spring breeze and had the scent of flowers in a summer's field. Suddenly Nikki was filled with a courage and confidence such as she had never known.

"Oh Eben-ezer!" Nikki cried out, flinging her arms around the ram's great neck. "I do know you!" The girl burrowed her head into the soft coat of the creature. "I do know you and I love you!"

"And I know you, my child." The ram spoke kindly to her. "And some day we shall dance on the Fields of Eternal Joy together. But for now you have a great mission before you."

Nikki pulled back from Eben-ezer.

"Oh, Eben-ezer. How are we ever going to defeat something as horrible as Apollyon and bring back our world?" the girl asked, sobbing.

"You shall defeat him because I have already defeated his master. Long ago, and within the Fields of Man I met with him in battle and placed him beneath me. And you have believed in me as you know me in your world. That is how you know me now.

"Apollyon has not really destroyed your true universe. It is a trick, a lie of the Evil One who was once the Anointed Cherub," the ram explained. "Five years ago, as you count time, that fallen cherub caused all of your universe to go off into a false reality. That is, reality was detoured, if you will, into a might-have-been. This was caused to happen because that devil realized he would never be able to release Apollyon from his prison within the realm of reality which my Father has established. All that which was destroyed was that might-have-been."

"Then my world still lives!" Nikki exclaimed.

"Not exactly," the ram continued. "For all the souls of the people within the Fields of Man were detoured into that might-have-been. When he destroyed it, all went with it."

"Then we're just as bad off as I thought at first," Nikki said darkly.

"Not at all," Eben-ezer corrected, "for the 'might-have-been' where you met Paul's mother is the real version of your universe. It only awaits your defeat of Apollyon so that I and my Father can restore to it the souls of all those of the Fields of Man."

"Then Paul's mother isn't dead!" Nikki exclaimed.

"No," Eben-ezer answered. "It was within the devil's detour that she was dead, not within the world of my Father's will. When you defeat the enemy, all will be as it should have been."

"But how do I defeat an archdemon who can wipe out an entire universe?"

"Remember me when the time comes," the ram said. "You will know what to do then."

"I don't understand," Nikki said, looking down at her feet. She felt ashamed that she did not know what the ram was trying to tell her.

"I am always with you, Nikki. Do not be afraid," the ram assured her.

"But I..." She looked up but there was no one there. "Where are you? Eben-ezer? Don't leave me now! I don't understand! Eben-ezer!"

"Nikki! Nikki, wake up!" Paul was shaking the girl who was crying out in her sleep.

"What? Where is he?" She sat up and looked about her. Again she was in the cabin of Tom Tit Tot. Everyone around her was awake, roused by her outcry.

"What is it, Nikki?" Old Joshua was beside her now.

"It's Eben-ezer! He's here. I was just talking to him!" she exclaimed.

"She's dreaming," Gwydion grumped. "Go back to sleep, child. We have a long day before us tomorrow."

"Yes, she was asleep," Old Joshua returned. "But perhaps she did meet Eben-ezer in her dreams. You know well that he speaks to us in dreams and visions when times are dire." Then to Nikki he said, "Go back to sleep, perhaps you will meet him again or perhaps not. Tomorrow we shall talk of what you have seen."

With that the girl stretched out again and soon all returned to the business of sleep.

When morning dawned the companions were awakened by the smell of breakfast coming from across the room, as Nonnie busied herself cooking on a great iron stove. The company arose and everyone took their turn washing up at the river. With all that out of the way, they all sat down to a great breakfast of eggs scrambled with cheese, fresh bread and pancakes with lots of wild berry syrup. When all had eaten their fill, Nonnie concerned herself with the chores of the home while Tom prepared his boat for the journey down river. Within two hours after breakfast the company found themselves waving their cheerful goodbyes to Nonnie, as Tom poled them out into the current for the journey downstream.

For three hours they rode the steady current downstream with only one minor incident when everyone had to hold on tight for a ride over a brief section of rapids. Now and again, Tom would call out a hello to some animal along the side of the bank and several times he called out to someone he evidently saw amongst the brush. The Children-of-Man saw no one on those occasions but figured he had seen some form of fairy-folk too shy to appear before a craft carrying the likes of them.

Nikki took the opportunity to relate her dream to the entire company. Paul was excited to find that the world in which his mother lived was the stream of reality which should have been, rather than being a might-have-been. After a long discussion of the subject, Old Joshua and Gwydion finally agreed that the dream was a vision and that Nikki and the entire fellowship should take heart from it and give thanks to El Elyon and Eben-ezer for their direction and blessings.

Tom told a number of stories of strange and wonderful passengers he had ferried up and down the river over the long Elfame years. Finally, however, all stories and tales had to come to an end as they neared the Cabbage Patches. Tom let the fellowship off at a little inlet only a few yards from the patches.

"I be thinking ye may need me further on, for as I see it ye'll be needing to travel on downriver in your quest," Tom told the company, as they unloaded their gear and packed up Zebedee. "If indeed the old hermit turns out to be this True Thomas ye seek, then when ye've finished business with him ye'll find me right here a'waitin."

The company made their way up the bank as Tom secured his boat in the inlet. They soon found themselves facing a huge cabbage patch which covered hundreds of yards in all directions. "Somebody sure likes sauerkraut from the looks of it," Harold quipped.

"Hush, boy!" Gwydion crabbed. "Cabbage patches and bean fields carry strong magic that can be worked by folk who know what they are about."

"What Gwydion says is true, Harold," Old Joshua added. "Let us see what we find across this expanse of cabbage. Everyone look lively, now! No missteps! We don't want anyone lost in a magic maze."

They moved carefully through the huge cabbage patch, all of them huddled together into a group so that no one would get separated. Strangely enough, to the thoughts of Gwydion and Joshua at least, they made it across the cabbage with no mishap whatsoever. There was a small grassy expanse after the cabbages and then a huge bean field twice the size of the cabbage patch. Here they drew up short.

"Now we take care," Gwydion said thoughtfully. "I sense some very strong magic in this field. No doubt if we go crashing about here carelessly, we'll all wake up several days hence, miles downstream, stupid as the day we were born."

The old wizard spent several long moments in deep thought before speaking again. He pulled Harold to his side by the boy's shoulder.

"Come here, my boy. It's time you started acting like a student of El Elyon," Gwydion said, and his tone of voice reminded Harold of the grumpy "merrroph's" the Cait Sidth would make to Old Joshua. The old wizard reached into his robe and produced a small leather-bound book which looked to be of great age. "Here, see what you can do with this."

Harold gingerly took the antique, eyes wide with the wonder of his mentor trusting him with one of his treasured items.

"What exactly do I do?" Harold asked, still looking down at the book.

"Well, it's a book, you ninny. I suppose you would want to open it up and try reading something," the old man spouted, his voice seemingly filled with exasperation at his young charge. "You learn a lot by reading, you know!"

"But where do I begin?" the boy puzzled.

"With that book, Harold," Gwydion's tone changed to one of calm assurance. "You cannot go wrong. Just open it up and try reading. Let the wisdom of El Elyon fill your spirit."

The boy tentatively opened the old volume. The feel of fine leather on his hands was accentuated by the smell of antiquity as he parted the pages about midway into the book. Silently, Harold began reading. Long moments he stood there; none of the company daring to speak, as he poured over the page he had opened to. Suddenly, a look of enlightenment lit his face.

"There is a great ward set about this field," he finally spoke.

"Yes, yes. I already know that, my boy!" Gwydion spoke with impatience. "Now what else do you discern?"

Harold read a bit further, then closed his eyes tightly for a moment.

"*Eli-a teash-ney, Keshna te-san'tee,*" Harold said, when he finally spoke. Then he continued, "Facing forward from whence you came, move ever back to your goal."

"That's it, my boy," Gwydion said calmly. "You have heard the wisdom of El Elyon. Now, do you know how to use it?"

"I think," Harold began slowly, "we should turn around and face the river. Then we should walk through the bean field backward. That will keep the enchantment of becoming lost from falling on us."

"Excellent! Excellent, my boy!" the old man shouted. "Joshua, we may make something useful from this whelp yet!"

Old Joshua gave Harold a hearty squeeze on the shoulder. "Yes, I believed from the first that he would be of The Spirit," he said. "Let us thank El Elyon for his blessing and be on with our journey."

Old Joshua gathered the fellowship about him and he sang an ancient and enchanting song of praise to El Elyon, and from it all could feel the Deep Magic flow. Then the company set out into the bean field, walking backward.

Carefully sighting a tree at the river's edge which could be seen past the cabbage patch, they made their way through the tangle of the bean vines. After about half an hour of artful maneuvering in reverse, the company emerged from the far side and into a clearing before a wooded glen.

Down the verdant slope of the glen they traveled across lush grass, with the moist earth giving beneath their feet. The smell of fresh earth came up to meet them and as they broke through the trees they caught sight of a neat little cottage with a man plowing a small field.

He looked up at the fellowship and called his pony to a halt, waving up at the party.

A feeling of joy came over Nikki, Paul and Harold. It was the feeling that they never wanted to leave this place. It was the feeling that each would be content to live out the rest of eternity right here on this small farm in the magical glen. Happily, they all walked down to the edge of the field where the man stood to meet them. He was a man of middle age and average height. He had a noble look about him which bespoke many years within the Fields of Elfame. He wore a simple brown shirt of cotton and brown breeches which came just below his knees. His feet were shod in soft moccasins. Upon his head was a wide brimmed hat, much like a fedora. The man smiled a broad and friendly smile.

"I am Thomas of Erceldoune, the Rhymer."
He extended a friendly hand to Old Joshua who was
in the lead of the party. "I have been expecting you.
In my dreams of last night, Eben-ezer told me of
your coming. Welcome, my friends."

CHAPTER XIII

Siege and Confrontation

*T*he soldiers on the walls of the palace of Gwyn ap Nudd had watched as the fellowship left the village. They were able to see them traveling down the road which led from the village toward the river Cellerdore, and each one knew that the hopes of all good folk within the Fields of Elfame depended upon the success of those travelers.

The day was a long one as soldiers awaited news of the approaching army, with everyone at his post and all drawn up to the walls in full battle

For hours they stood the heat of the Elfame sun, soldiers sweating inside brass helmets and plate armor.

Banners flapped lazily in the slight breeze as if a carnival were in town, but the sounds of merriment were absent from the scene. Grim faces lined the walls. The drawbridge was down and a full company manned the barbican as a first defense against the as-yet-unseen enemy. With little noise, women in the courtyard prepared equipment that would be needed during the battle. Engines of war were tested and made ready for the upcoming fight.

Now and again the rattle and clash of a catapult would break the stillness, as artillery men tested their distance and accuracy upon the empty field before them. From deeper within the city came an occasional roar and crash as great trebuchets were test-fired.

Then, at noon, it happened.

The cry rang out from the northernmost tower and all eyes turned toward the northwest. The horizon had become a black, waving line. It seemed that the very horizon line seemed to waver from the marching. Slowly the mass of dark creatures advanced, and by two hours past noon their army could be seen filling the plain before the onlookers. It was a massive army which moved on Gwyn ap Nudd.

The king himself was upon the north wall in full battle armor. He had many high fairies from times ancient with him. Like him, they could remember distant eons, times when their people had fought the powers of evil in the name of El Elyon. A few of them were old enough to remember their grandparents tell of the great war at time's start. It was they who would weave the deep magic of the Creator in hopes of shielding the palace from the greater brunt of the assault. But none knew what power of devils the dark army brought, which could undo their magic.

By the time night fell the massive army was all about. Harsh horns blasted and torches bobbed by the thousands as the dark army surrounded all approachable sections of the city, in preparation of attack. Within an hour after dark, fires had sprung up within the village at the foot of the palace hill.

"They're burning the village!" The cry went forth along the wall. It was picked up in the city and carried deep into the palace where the young and women were safetied away. Many hearts of the younger ones sank as the news of the burning village reached them. The ones on the wall brushed it off as a mere aside to the terrors which were about to befall them.

* * *

"So you are really True Thomas," Paul said, as he raised his mug for a long drink of cold apple cider. "We read just about every account of you before we came over here to Elfame." "Indeed," Thomas returned in his thick Irish brogue. "Won't you have another cake, Nikki? They're freshly baked, you know."

Everyone was seated about on the porch of Thomas' cabin and eating fresh honey cakes and fruit and drinking cold apple juice. Zebedee was in the small barn out back with Jack, the pony of True Thomas.

"Then, from all accounts, that would make you hundreds of years old," Harold said, between bites of a large red apple.

"About seven hundred as you count time, my boy," Thomas answered. "I left the Fields of Man long ago. It would have been the Thirteenth Century and I have been here ever since."

"You don't look like you could be a day over fifty. How can that be?" Nikki questioned. "But I already know the answer to that one. Time moves differently here than in the Fields of Man."

Everyone around the porch chuckled as Nikki made a funny face at herself while answering her own obvious question. Finally, everyone settled down to a serious discussion of the problem at hand. Thomas told the story of the Sleeping Warriors in greater detail than had any of the books of Gwydion and Joshua. He recounted the events of earlier wars between Elfame and the Anointed Cherub, "the Devil himself," as Thomas insisted on calling him. After several hours of these accounts, along with lengthy discussion and questions from Gwydion and Joshua, Thomas came to the most important part.

"Now, the matter which faces you is to know exactly where to look for the warriors," Thomas said. "They lie within a mound on Skye Isle. To get there you'll have to go by sea, but it is a short journey and the way is prepared for you. There is another matter which presents a problem, however – the key to the mound has been stolen."

"Oh, that's just bloody wonderful!" Gwydion spouted.

"How on earth are we going to get into the mound if we don't have the key?" Nikki asked, jumping to her feet in excitement. "Don't tell me we have come all this way, across dimensions and fighting demons only to find that we can't even get to the one source that will save us!"

"Simply put, you will have to recover the key," Thomas explained, as Paul put out a steadying hand to Nikki. "And although that will not be easy, it will be no harder than the other obstacles you have already cleared."

"How do we go about getting the key back?" Harold asked.

"You will have to defeat the creature who now holds it," Thomas answered. "You see, long ago a smith who lived in the area of the mound decided he would enter it and investigate. He examined the keyhole and was successful in making a key which would fit it. This move almost broke the enchantment, since there was to be no key made until the time of the rising of the warriors. Luckily, the deep magic of El Elyon is greater than any other. Anyway, the smith went to the mound and opened the door. When he entered he discovered the warriors, dread and terrible, all lying about on their biers. He took hold of the horn and gave a mighty blast. At this, the warriors began to stir and rise and a great spirit of fear fell over the place. The smith was so terrified that he fled, slamming the door behind him, and threw the key into a lake."

"So why don't we just have another key made?" Paul asked.

"That is part of the problem," Thomas replied. "Only one key could ever be made, and it was supposed to be made by me. The key was later discovered by a kelpie, a treacherous water demon. It is now guarded by him in the hopes that no one will ever be able to open the mound and free the warriors."

"Oh, that's just great. We get to fight another demon!" Nikki shouted. "Why can't these things ever be little creatures – pushovers?"

"Hush, my child," Gwydion groused. Then he turned to Thomas. "Just where do we go about finding this kelpie?"

"That is the easy part," Thomas answered.

"I was afraid you were going to say something like that," Nikki moaned. "But I guess it has to be done."

"Very true, Nikki," Thomas said. "And to answer your question, Gwydion, the kelpie dwells on the very river you are traveling."

"Good!" Gwydion interjected.

"Good?" Harold questioned.

"Of course, my boy!" the old man returned. "This way we don't have to go traipsing all over creation looking for him. This will make our job a whole lot easier."

"Now," Thomas began again, "downriver some miles from here you will come to a sharp bend. There is a great rock wall in the corner of that bend and this causes a whirlpool which makes navigation quite a feat. The kelpie has his lair therein and charges a toll to any who wish to pass up or down the river. It is said he has amassed a considerable fortune from collecting tolls all these years. And among his treasures — the key! Defeat him in combat and you can have it all."

"Just what does this kelpie look like?" Nikki asked.

"Oh, he is horrible indeed!" Thomas returned. "The creature has a horse body from the waist down and from the waist up he has the body of a man, but for the head. The head is that of a grotesque fanged horse. The beast is a cannibal and will eat any victim who challenges and loses."

Plans were then made and the afternoon meal was taken with Thomas before the company collected Zebedee from the barn and repacked him for the river.

"You will have no problem getting back through the bean field," Thomas told them. "It is only enchanted to keep people out. Walk through it without fear upon leaving. There is one more thing I must tell you about the mound of the warriors, however."

"And what would that be?" Joshua asked.

"You must use the words that I will tell you when you turn the key in the lock," he said. "Otherwise dread will overtake you as you work the three enchantments in the mound of the Sleeping Warriors.

"Remember now — when the key is in the lock you must call out, 'In the name of the Lamb, in the way of the Lion, by the power of innocent blood!' Upon doing this, and only this, the door of the mound must be opened."

"Then, once inside, one of us must draw the sword, cut the garter and blow a blast on the horn. Right?" Nikki asked.

"And the warriors will arise," Thomas answered. "You will then be told what must be done to defeat Apollyon. The warriors will ride off to destroy the black armies which even now attack the palace of Gwyn ap Nudd. You must not be delayed in your journey, however, for the palace cannot stand for many days against the enemy."

Thomas then reached into a pocket and pulled out a small silver whistle which was hung from a cord. He handed it to Nikki.

"If you are successful in your fight with the kelpie and take the key," said Thomas to Nikki, "you must make your way on down the river to the sea. There, upon the sands of the sea, blow this whistle and await its answer. As I told you earlier, your trip across the sea to Skye Island has long been prepared for."

Nikki took the whistle, a look of awe in her eyes at its intricately carved beauty. Silently, she hung it about her neck, then looked back up at Thomas.

"Thank you," she said. "And while we journey, pray for us that El Elyon will send Eben-ezer to guard us and that we will succeed in our quest. All of creation depends on us! And we have so little time left, what with the palace already under attack and our world gone."

Thomas leaned forward and whispered something in Nikki's ear then turned and walked back to his porch. With that the company departed the glen of True Thomas, climbing up through the woods and across to the bean field where they made their way back to the river where Tom Tit Tot awaited them.

"What did Thomas whisper to you before we left?" Paul asked, as they climbed back onto the raft.

"That was strange," she answered. "He said, 'The sword is the road and the lamp which out-shone Antiochus. You must plant it for the salvation of all!' What do you suppose he meant?"

Siege and Confrontation

* * *

Throughout the night the soldiers on the palace walls fought. The first wave of the black army hit with the force of a tsunami. Thousands scaled the hillside as the first onslaught began. New stars seemed to form every few minutes as fiery arrows rained down upon the city. It was only the magic of the king and his Ancients-of-the-Deep-Magic which kept the fiery onslaught from wreaking havoc upon the defenders. With each rain of fire there sprang up a shield-web over the city which turned the flaming missiles into harmless ash as they passed through. Still, it took the enemy a full two hours before they gave up the effort.

The soldiers defending the barbican did not fare as well, however. The enemy assailed the fortification with scaling ladders and battering rams, and the fire arrows took their toll there. Just prior to dawn the barbican fell. The great doors finally yielded to the destructive might of the great rams. With a resounding crash they buckled and burst inward with an explosion of splinters. The enemy was inside.

The fairy-soldiers fought bravely but to no avail, finally having to give up the fortification and retreat across the drawbridge to the relative safety of the city walls. The great bridge was raised just as the last of the fighters was safely inside. The flames from the fallen barbican danced ghostlike across the faces of the soldiers fighting from the city walls.

With dawn the enemy pulled back, leaving the blackened ruins of the barbican still smoldering. Battle-weary warriors drew deep sighs of relief; some sank to the floor in exhaustion as the evil hordes withdrew. The day was just dawning, though, and the enemy was only pulling back to catch its breath and prepare for its second onslaught.

* * *

"Be quiet now as you look," Tom Tit Tot said as he parted the brush. Through it could be seen a sharp bend in the river, some hundred feet ahead. It was backed by a stone cliff, and the center of the bend was torn by a huge whirlpool.

"Yes, I see," Fionn whispered to the gnome. Tom had put his boat into shore about half a mile back, and he and the fairy-warrior had scouted ahead. "It looks impossible to take by surprise," Fionn added, after a moment's scrutiny.

No sooner had he spoken than the waters near the wall began to boil and froth, and from their churning midst rose a most hideous sight. It was a massive creature, mostly shaped like a man but with the head and lower body of a nightmarish horse. Out of the water it sprang and onto the wide rock shore which ran along the base of the stone cliff.

Tom and Fionn were perfectly still as only fairy-creatures can be. Still, the creature turned, sniffing in their direction. In a moment, it seemed to locate them. With eyes burning red like the fires of hell, it leveled a clawed finger toward them.

"I smell you there, hiding from the inevitable!" the great voice boomed. "I will advance not upon you but mark these words. If you intend passing you shall surely pay my toll or face the challenge of battle with me. Now begone until you can decide which it will be!"

"I suppose that settles that," Tom said in a normal voice, now that the threat of discovery and death was no longer hanging over them.

"Then it's back to the company to let the Children-of-Man decide our course," Fionn returned.

They rose from their hiding place into full view of the monster at river's bend. "When you have made your decision, ferishers," the monster boomed again, "I will be here. Perhaps I shall pick my teeth with your bones!"

"I don't know about you," Tom began, as he backed away from the sight of the kelpie, "but I don't like the plans he has for us."

"Let him plan all he wants," Fionn boasted, turning his back to the demon and beginning his walk back to where the companions waited. "He has not met our company yet, and besides, the blessings of Eben-ezer are upon our journey."

Together they made their way back up the river where the fellowship greeted them, eager to discover what they had learned.

Old Joshua thought it best to wait until the morrow to attack, but Gwydion felt it best to take up the challenge at once. The two fell into an hour's discussion until Gwydion won out with his usual sour-natured persistence. When they stopped to take ideas as to just how the challenge was to be presented, and by whom, they noticed for the first time since the two old wizards had fallen to arguing that Nikki was nowhere about.

"Where is she?" Paul shouted, as he turned to and fro looking for Nikki.

"I know where she is!" Harold returned. The boy was busy tucking the Hammer of St. Dunstan into his belt. He then took off down the path along the riverbank, toward the demon's lair.

"The child has gone to face the monster alone," Old Joshua realized aloud.

"This would not have happened if you had not been so eager to dispute, you old poot!" Gwydion shouted at Joshua. "She slipped away when my attention was on your silly argument!"

"Come on!" Paul interjected hotly. "There's no time for that now. We've got to stop her, if it's not already too late." With that he was off, running down the path after Harold, who was already out of sight.

Paul caught up with Harold just as the younger boy reached the brush from which Fionn and Tom had sighted the monster. He drew up short behind Harold and the two stared wide-eyed at the scene playing before them. Nikki was standing face to face with the hideous horse-man demon, not a hundred feet in front of them. The sound of their debate was projected with perfect clarity from the cliff walls to where the two young men stood as the others of the company caught up.

"Give me the key bogey beast, and I will leave you alone!" Nikki shouted at the horse-monster.

"Nikki, no." Old Joshua's voice was but a whisper as he pushed between Harold and Paul for a better view.

"You little fool!" the kelpie bellowed at the girl. "You think me no more than a common bogey beast such as roams these fields? I will rend you limb from limb!"

"Give me the key now and save yourself," Nikki stated flatly.

The demon's eyes narrowed in contemplation. Did this slip of a girl know some magic he was
not aware of? He pondered the thought for a moment before giving it up as ridiculous.

"I will chew your pretty little body to bloody
pulp!" the creature raged, stirred by the girl's defiance. "You are so fond of that precious little body
of yours, are you not?"

"I am warning you, demon," Nikki spoke, ignoring the creature's threat. "Deal with me in peace
or I shall leave you in torment!"

"What is she doing?" Gwydion queried.

"Quiet, friend," Old Joshua said, holding up a
silencing hand. "I believe I know what she is doing.
She has realized her birthright!"

"But surely that creature will rend her asunder," Phadrig said. The Phouka had moved to
Gwydion's side.

"And what torment do you propose to leave me
in?"

"I know the secret of Eben-ezer," Nikki stated
with finality.

"Ha!" the demon spat. "And what do you know
of that yellow sheep that will save you? You are no
more than a vain, over-sexed little slut from a world
that no longer stands! Even on your best days your
only thoughts were of how close to naked your laws

would allow you to be on the beach. Your greatest thrill was to give cheap sexual rushes to the suckling boys of your world by means of scant dress and what you call your Hollywood image! You are not worth a second glance from your God!"

"Those things are true, perhaps," came Nikki's reply. "But my sins are covered by innocent blood, and before that you cannot stand."

"Stupid, brazen little fool!" the demon screamed. "It was you and your kind who killed him. Do not toss your 'innocent blood' at my door-step!" The monster took a step back from Nikki.

"You had your chance, demon," Nikki spoke coldly.

"No!" The monster shouted. "You're making a mistake! This is only an illusion. Look, I reveal my true self to you!"

With that the demon began to shimmer and in a moment's time was transformed into a shining angel of light. The radiance of his beauty flashed about the cliff walls and dazzled the swirling waters.

"See, Nikki, my dear." The transformed demon spoke in a voice honey sweet. "I am of the Elohim, the Sons of God. I will not harm you if you place your trust in me."

"Do you think that I am so stupid I can't see through this vision of your former self?" Nikki asked.

"You may have appeared in this form eons ago but you fell when you followed the Anointed Cherub in his rebellion."

"Just trust in me," the demon continued. "Look, I will give you riches beyond your wildest dreams!" With a wave of his hand, the demon stopped the whirlpool, and at the bottom of the river there came into sight the gleam of gold and jewels collected by the creature over the centuries.

"Enough of this foolishness," Nikki said coldly. "I know your name and it is *Deceiver!*"

"No!" the creature cried out.

"And I banish you," Nikki continued. "By the innocent blood of the Lion-Lamb I condemn you to wander in a dry place until the day of your judgment!"

"NO!" The angel-beast's scream was a pathetic cry of the damned. He writhed for a moment, as if wrapped in invisible flames. Then in a burst of smoke and a flash of light he was gone and a golden key fell, ringing like a chime against the rock where the demon had stood.

"She did it!" Paul leapt from the brush and made a dash for Nikki.

"She did it." Old Joshua turned his smile toward the other members of the fellowship. "She has discovered her birthright, it is that of all..."

Before he could finish, a mighty roar split the air and echoed from the cliff walls. Paul had just reached Nikki. He had her in his arms and was swinging her around joyously when the roar burst forth.

All eyes turned toward the uppermost crags of the cliff. There, upon its highest point, stood the great golden form of Eben-ezer. The mighty golden ram roared like a triumphant lion, then smiled down at the assembled fellowship. His eyes flashed with power but as his gaze fell on one after the other of the fellowship, each found themselves filled with a deep feeling of peace and love.

"Well done, my children," the mighty ram spoke. His voice was powerful yet soft. It gave the feeling that with the slightest effort his words could strike an enemy to the ground, or heal the gravest wound. "But you must hurry on your mission. There is much to be done and time grows short."

With that the great golden ram turned and leapt from the pinnacle where he had stood. In an instant his mighty form had disappeared amongst the thicket at cliff's top.

CHAPTER XIV

The Turning Of The Worm

*N*ikki stood ankle deep in the sea as it rolled about her feet. As the sun rose over the eastern sea she blew the silver whistle given to her by True Thomas. Now, for over an hour, she had stood motionless, waiting. The landward sea breeze slicked her diaphanous fairy-tunic against her and her golden sandals made her feet feel like they wanted to float as the salt water washed around them.

High and behind the girl, Phadrig's black form was silhouetted against the morning sky, as he stood upon a sea cliff, next to a tall waterfall which had ended the river's journey to the sea. His sharp eyes scanned the horizon for — he knew not what. Joshua, Paul, Tom and the two fairies sat on the beach around a small fire they had kindled against the morning's chill. Harold, with the large white form of the Cait Sidth in his arms, walked out to meet his sister as she stood in the sea foam. Gwydion had changed back into the form of the Cait Sidth following the encounter with the kelpie. He had said his eyes and ears would be sharper for use on the venture, but it was Harold's thought that the old wizard was feeling bad about the argument which preceded Nikki's encounter with the water demon. The lad thought that this was the old wizard's way of sulking without being a total grouch to his companions, what with a grumpy cat being a lot easier to take than a crotchety old wizard.

"Anything yet, Sis?" the boy asked, as he waded up to Nikki. The girl made no reply, choosing only to shake her head slowly as she stared into the mornings gray sea mist.

"Merrr-uph!" the cat in Harold's arms snarled.

"No, Gwydion, she's not sulking," Harold answered the Cait Sidth.

"You can understand him?" Nikki broke her silence at this, and turned her head to face her brother.

"Can't you?" Harold returned.

"Sure, I just don't know what 'Merrr-uph' means in English," she quipped.

"Reee-owph!" the cat growled.

"And that?" Nikki queried.

"He said not to be silly, that of course I can understand him," the boy replied.

"I'll be glad when..." Nikki's comment was cut short by Phadrig's cry from atop the sea cliff.

"A ship!" The cry carried down from where the Phouka stood. "A ship of the Gwragedd Annwn, the sea fairies! And coming this way!"

* * *

Midmorning brought a renewal of the enemy's attack on the palace. The warriors on the walls found the attack of the night before to have been a simple test for the young warriors. Now the combat-hardened troops faced the real battle.

The clatter of the enemy's catapults rattled over the cries of battle. The steady pounding of their heavy missiles against the city walls punctuated the fears of the women and the young. If not for the deep magic of the king and his ancients, the walls would not have held an hour against such an attack.

On several occasions, long scaling ladders were floated into the moat and stood up in the water, which had successfully allowed Red Caps onto the battlements. Each time this happened the fighting became hand-to-hand. It was savage and bloody, but the fairy-troops managed to turn each successful scaling of the walls into victory for their side. By mid-afternoon a thousand Red Caps were dead — strewn about the walls, floating in the moat and scattered about the hillside before the palace.

Then came the giants.

They towered twenty feet tall, and wore iron armor. They lumbered up the hillsides, carrying great stone axes. They paused long enough at the ruins of the barbican to level it with their axes before moving on to wade the moat.

There were five of them and the arrows of the archers ricocheted off their armor like pebbles off iron. The king's magicians wove many spells about the gates, but as the afternoon wore on, one after another gave way to the relentless smashing.

Finally, as dusk was falling, the floor of the drawbridge splintered. The giants ripped and pulled at the structure until the bridge was torn from its workings and flung over the wall where it landed in a city courtyard. The iron portcullis was now the only thing between the enemy and the oak doors of the city, and the giants quickly began wrenching at these.

Weariness was beginning to overtake the king's magicians, and as the bars of the portcullis began to groan, the king ordered all the oil within the city to be brought to the forward wall.

Quickly, huge vats of oil were moved to the wall where they were dumped over the attacking giants. Torches were then tossed and the giants turned from an attacking terror to a raging inferno of bellowing pain. They struggled to get free of the fiery oil but it floated all about the moat. Blinded by the flames and in pain as they roasted within their own iron armor, the giants began one by one to sink into the flaming waters. Within twenty minutes the flames were out and only one giant was left alive. He had managed to get to shore where he crawled out, nearly burned to death. For a moment he attempted to pull himself up and crawl toward his army, but a catapult shot from his own side smashed into his head, dealing a final blow.

As night fell about them, the black army again rethought their strategy to mount a new attack.

* * *

"A ship?" Old Joshua was on his feet and running toward Nikki and Harold, with Paul and the fairies close at his heels. Phadrig bounded down the path from the cliff top.

The companions watched from the shore as the fairy-ship cut deftly through the misty sea. Its golden prow cleaved the waves, and its silver-trimmed sky-blue sail billowed full in the wind. Within only minutes from its sighting, the company could make out sailors on board working to take in the sails. Soon the ship was anchored a hundred yards from shore and a small silver dinghy was launched. It carried four passengers.

Standing foremost in the prow of the boat were a tall, silver-haired fairy man and a woman. They were dressed in flowing blue robes and girdled in silver. Behind them, two fairy-seamen pulled at the oars, making the little boat move like an arrow on the water, following the rolling surf to the shore. Never once did the two on the prow waver or lose their footing.

Within moments from having put out, the silver dinghy was beached and the two seamen jumped out to pull it high onto the dry sand before the gathered fellowship. The man and woman remained on the little boat, looking very like lord and lady of the sea itself. The two were as beautiful, or more so, as any the Children-of-Man had encountered in the land of Tir Nan Og. They shimmered in a silver aura which rose and fell in intensity with the rhythm of the sea.

Directed by instinct, Nikki stepped forward, removing the silver whistle from around her neck. She handed it to the two in the boat. The man reached to receive it, and smiled sweetly at Nikki as he did so.

"I am the Lord Barathane." He broke the silence as he received the whistle. "And this is my wife, the Lady Shalladill. We have waited long for this signal."

"With glad hearts we welcome your company," the woman added. "Come now and enter our boat so that we may carry you to the Isle of Skye where you will fulfill your destiny."

Lord Barathane extended his hand to Nikki, who accepted it and stepped lightly onto the silver boat.

"Come," he beckoned to the others. "In the name of Eben-ezer, the Lion-Lamb, I bid you welcome." His words seemed to lift a weight from the hearts of the company, and one by one they began to climb aboard the dinghy. The little silver boat seemed to grow slightly with each person and all fit easily within its enchanted hull. Even Zebedee the pony was readily accommodated.

At last only Tom Tit Tot and Phadrig remained on the beach. "Come on!" Nikki encouraged the two. A feeling of pure joy had overcome her the moment she stepped into the little boat and she smiled brightly toward her two friends on the beach.

"I am afraid that I must be returning upriver to my Nonnie," Tom replied, as he returned Nikki's smile. "I paddle my little boat up and down the river, but it is not for me to go sailing about the sea on ships and such. We will pray blessings on your trip and await your triumphant return."

"Phadrig?" Nikki asked, a hint of sadness creeping into her heart, as she knew already what the Phouka's reply would be.

"My dear Nikki," the fairy-beast answered, "I have come to love you and all the others deeply, yet I too must remain behind. I join my prayers with Tom and Nonnie and together we shall await your return. Be brave in the spirit of Eben-ezer and your mission. The blessings of El Elyon be upon you all."

With that the great fairy-beast turned and began walking back toward the cliff path. The two fairy-seamen began to shove off and within moments they were riding the waves away from the shore. Shortly after, the fellowship found themselves on the deck of the Mist Cleaver, watching the shores of Tir Nan Og disappear into the mist of morning.

Hours passed as Nikki watched the sea slip beneath the prow of the Mist Cleaver. By noon the sea had cleared and a steady breeze carried them on a northeasterly course.

"Look, there are dolphins!" shouted Harold, who stood next to his sister on the prow. Nikki looked in the direction Harold indicated, and sure enough, dolphins were leaping and racing alongside the ship's port side.

"Oh, they're beautiful!" Nikki exclaimed, her thoughts returning from their wanderings. She rushed to the side to get a better look.

"They are our friends," one of the fairy-seamen said. He was working some rope into neat coils and had stopped to watch the dolphins. "We are fast friends with the good folk of the sea."

"I wish I could talk to dolphins," Nikki mused.

"That is a kind thought," said the sailor. "I'll tell them you said so." With that, the fairy pursed his lips and whistled shrilly. He then gave several high pitched calls from the back of his throat. At this, one of the dolphins leapt into the air, turning a complete somersault. It leapt again, this time giving a shrill chatter, then tail-walked backwards for several feet before disappearing to rejoin his companions in their race with the ship.

Harold laughed with joy at the dolphin's antics.

"Did he say something?" Nikki quickly asked.

"He returns your greeting and says that in heaven we shall all speak with one tongue!" the sailor answered, with a smile.

Paul stepped out onto the deck from below where he had been exploring the ship. He stretched in the warm sunlight, then headed over to where Nikki stood.

"Joshua and the others still talking with Barathane?" he asked.

"Yes," she answered, and then with great animation said, "Paul, look at the dolphins. One of them just spoke to me!"

Paul was about to inquire as to how exactly this conversation with dolphins had transpired, but he was interrupted by the call "Land ho!" from the lookout.

"That will be the Isle of Skye," said the sailor who had spoken to the dolphins for Nikki. "You are near the end of your quest, Children-of-Man."

At the cry of land, Lord Barathane, Lady Shalladill and the rest of the company came from the main cabin, which rode high on the stern of the ship. Nikki, Paul and Harold could see them pointing and looking in the direction that the lookout had indicated. The Children could not hear the conversation but it looked as if some matters of great concern were being discussed.

"I wonder what they are up to?" said Paul.

"Probably getting directions to the mound," Harold returned. "The sea fairies seem to be in the know about our quest."

The sailors made ready for putting to at the isle and the deck came alive with their activity. There was little time for Nikki, Harold and Paul to wonder further, for they were quickly put to work by the fairy-seamen. They carried supply boxes then coiled ropes and loaded them into the dinghy, and otherwise lent a hand with the minor things of seamanship that they could handle. Within an hour the sails were being struck.

The island loomed large on the horizon now and the fellowship gathered on the main deck as the silver dinghy was prepared. Soon the anchor was dropped and the Lord and Lady of the ship again escorted them into the landing craft. The little silver boat skimmed the waves, carrying them onto a sandy white beach. The fairies had given them provisions to continue their journey, and these were now loaded onto Zebedee, who seemed to have fared no ill from his sea journey.

When everyone had shouldered their loads, goodbyes were said and the fellowship made ready for what all hoped was the last leg of their journey.

"Remember my saying, Counselor," Lord Barathane called as the silver boat moved back into the surf. "Beware the 'worm, Chuian. He has haunted these parts for the last hundred years now!" His voice trailed off into the roar of the surf as the boat moved away.

"Whoa! Wait just a minute," Harold exclaimed. "What is this 'worm Chuian' and why haven't we heard about this before now?"

"Merrr-ouph! Meeeowww," Gwydion replied.

"What do you mean 'just a dragon'!" The boy snatched the Cait Sidth up by the shoulders. The big white cat spat and kicked with his hind legs, scratching Harold, who then quickly dropped the cat.

"What's he talking about?" Harold spun on Old Joshua.

"A dragon," Old Joshua answered.

"A dragon?" Nikki and Paul shouted, simultaneously.

Fionn and Eilian were silent. Old Joshua raised his hands to silence the them.

"Do not worry..." the old man began.

"Don't worry!" Harold interrupted. "Now we have to face a bloody dragon and you stand there telling us not to worry?"

"Reow!" Gwydion snarled at Harold, who was unslinging his pack.

"I don't know anything at all about magic," the boy said, answering the cat's snarl. "Maybe a few tricks you have managed to teach me here and there, but nothing to face something like a dragon with!"

"Harold," Old Joshua again tried. "Remember the demon and how we thought it would be a nasty fight? Nikki had him figured out before we even knew what we were doing."

"That's right," Paul agreed, getting into the spirit of the matter. "We've all grown up on stories about dragons but can it really be any worse than facing a demon?"

Harold only snorted.

"And besides," Nikki added, "what choice do we have? If we fail, the world is gone for good. So what if we die or are eaten or something? At least we died trying!" "Well..." Harold looked his sister in the eyes, the distress dying in his face. "I guess you're right. I'm sorry, okay?"

He knelt next to the Cait Sidth.

"I'm sorry I blew my top, okay?"

The Cait Sidth "murphed" and rubbed around the boy's leg. He then looked up at Harold, laid his ears back and spat a hiss.

"Okay," Harold said, raising his hands in surrender. "Now, what is this about a dragon?"

Joshua and the fairies told the rest of the company about the conversation held in Lord Barathane's cabin. Much of it had been about the worm Chuian.

"It seems the worm has lived here and about the lands of Elfame for ages," Joshua said. "About a hundred years ago it came here to this Isle of Skye."

"It flew in from the east," added Eilian. "I have heard stories about the beast."

"Yes," Joshua continued. "It spent some time terrorizing neighboring islands and the coastal areas after arriving from the east, but disappeared about a century ago. The sea fairies have kept track of the creature, noting that it has not moved from Skye for reasons unknown. They have left matters alone rather than do anything that would again arouse the creature. No one seems to know what the beast wants. It has been known to descend on villages and demand the answer to strange riddles. When no one can give an answer, the beast loots and burns the village. And so it goes."

"Let's hope we can steer clear of him. Let's get our job done and get out of here," Harold said.

Conversation continued on the subject of the dragon as the company started off. They moved up the coast until they found a path from the beach up into the interior of the isle. As they traveled, they discussed the bits and pieces of information given by the sea fairies about Chuian, trying to discover what could be motivating the creature.

By nightfall they had reached far inland and were beginning to pass from forest into a rocky, hilly country. For safety's sake, they decided to camp at the edge of the forest before starting into the more open countryside on the morrow.

By sunup they were all awake and finished with a good breakfast from the supplies provided by Lord Barathane's people. As the sun rose over the isle, they headed into the hills before them.

"According to the information we have," Joshua began, as they paused about mid-morning for a rest, "the Mound of the Sleeping Warriors should be straight through there. We could be there about this time tomorrow." He pointed directly across a group of low lying, rocky mountains.

"If we keep on moving at this rate, we should reach those mountains by noon," Fionn said.

"I wish we had horses," Nikki commented. "I want to get there as soon as possible."

"We would never be able to get horses through there," Joshua said, indicating the mountains.

Following a brief rest they were back on the march, and true enough, they were just into the mountains by noon. They were worn old mountains of a soft shale which broke and crumbled beneath their tread. Carefully they made their way upward, as little landslides formed from each member's footsteps. This made traveling more difficult than the company had expected and made the Children-of-Man glad for the help they got from their fairy-made footwear. Then about an hour after noon a slight wind picked up. It whipped up the dust from their steps and added to the difficulty of traveling. About fifteen minutes later they came into an area sheltered from the wind by high walls. Here they stopped and made lunch.

After lunch everyone stretched out for a short time of rest before picking up the journey. That is, everyone took a rest except Nikki.

"I'm too restless to nap," she announced. "I think I'll walk around here a little bit and see what I can find."

"Do not go far, Nikki," Old Joshua cautioned. "We cannot have you getting lost or hurt at this late point of our quest." "I'll be careful," she said, and was off.

For several minutes, Nikki clambered about the rocky terrain, glad again for the fairy-sandals she wore. Her intent was to climb up onto one of the nearby peaks in hopes of seeing across the mountains to their destination. She was moving toward a particularly interesting formation of rock, and as she neared it she slipped and skinned her knee.

"Ow! Durn, that hurts!" she exclaimed, as she sat down to pick little pieces of shale from her knee. It was not a very bad scrape, but her sweat made it sting.

"Just what exactly are you looking for?" a voice called out, from behind her. Nikki jumped to her feet and spun around, nearly buying a ride down a small slope covered in loose shale. As she caught her balance, she saw the "very interesting formation of rock" she had been heading for, uncoiling. Great bat-like wings began to unfurl and a hideous serpentine head reared, not twenty feet away from her.

Nikki screamed bloody murder, as surprise and fear overtook her.

The dragon cocked its head, and a wry grin appeared over its features.

"That's Nikki!" Paul shouted. Everyone leapt to their feet as if their legs were spring-loaded. "Ramph!" Gwydion yeowed, and was off like a shot.

"Yes, I'm coming as fast as I can!" Harold answered, following the white Cait Sidth. By the time the company reached Nikki, the dragon was standing in full glory before her. It towered over the jagged peaks where it had been resting, and the wind ruffled its membranous wings. These wings arched like a great gray canopy over the scene. Nikki was frozen in her tracks, and at first sight of the dragon the others also were seized by a powerfully paralyzing fear. None were able to move or to avert their eyes from the hypnotic gaze of the great worm.

"Strange," the dragon said, before his petrified audience. "Children-of-Man walking the Fields of Elfame. I suppose you have come in search of me, no?"

"Actually," Nikki said, having found her voice, "we were hoping to meet just about anything BUT you."

"What?" The worm drew back as if shocked. "You must have known I was here and have come looking to do battle with me."

"Believe me," Nikki was quick to answer, "you are not one of our concerns. We are on a very important quest and it has absolutely nothing to do with battling dragons."

"I see," said the dragon. "And what might this very important quest be, my pretty?"

"We are on a mission to save the world of man," Nikki stated, matter-of-factly. "So you see, we

want nothing to do with you and would like it very much if you would just let us pass."

"Oh, I see," the dragon said, again. "And what makes you think that I would wish to do that?" He then added rhetorically, "Do you have any idea what I could do with a fair maiden like yourself?"

"Now just a darn minute, here!" Paul found his voice and stepped forward to Nikki's defense.

"SILENCE!" the dragon bellowed at Paul. The blast of the creature's voice caused the company to step back several paces and cover their ears. "Do not make me angry. Believe me, it would not be in line with your best interests."

"Look." Nikki ventured another attempt. "We are only interested in our quest. I know that you are much more powerful than we are and that you could eat us all at any moment you chose. It's stupid for us to go on like this, so either let us go or go ahead and eat us where we stand. If we fail in our mission we may as well be eaten!"

"You are a brash little wench, are you not?" the dragon said, then it chuckled deeply. "Now, let me see just how intelligent you are. Answer me this, if you can:

> Born of mountain's heart,
> Forged in fire smart.
> Double mouthed, single toothed.

Drinker of blood, eater of souls.
Lives in cavern swung at side.
What am I?"

Old Joshua suddenly stepped forward. He adjusted his robe and looked up at the towering dragon.

"Is this supposed to be a tricky riddle?" the wizard asked. "If so, you are not as good as I have heard."

"Oh, so you finally admit you have heard of me?" the dragon returned.

"Why yes, we have heard of you," Joshua said. "It is just that we did not come looking for you."

"Well, either way, you found me and here we are," the dragon said. "So let me hear the answer, since it is so simple."

"What is born in the mountain's heart and forged in fire, but steel?" Old Joshua began. "A fang is for piercing and a mouth is the ancient term for an edge. It swings in a cavern, or scabbard, and is a double-edged sword. What else drinks the blood of battles and devours the soul of its victim?"

"Well, well, well." The dragon perked up with attention. "For the first time in ages, it seems I have the company of truly intelligent beings. You are the first to answer one of my riddles in time forgotten!" The dragon howled gleefully.

"If you do not mind my asking," said Old Joshua, "why do you find it necessary to go about asking riddles and rampaging madly about when your quarry cannot answer? What sort of sport is that?"

"It is not sport," the dragon returned. "It is necessity." "I don't understand why it would be necessary to go about burning and terrorizing innocent fairies," Nikki said.

The dragon turned his fiery gaze toward the girl. "No one is innocent within the realms of creation, beyond the throne of El Elyon!" the dragon bellowed. Nikki drew back a step.

"But if it is any concern of yours, or even within your comprehension, I am seeking a truth."

"What is this truth you seek?" Old Joshua asked, stepping to Nikki's side.

"I do not know why I should waste time telling you puny creatures," the dragon returned. "I usually couch my questions in riddles. But for now, I find it pleases me to speak frankly with you," the worm Chuain condescended. "Since you did answer my riddle straight off.

"The Anointed Cherub fell, along with one third of the Elohim of the Heavens. I do not see how they justly can be cast out, with no hope of forgiveness, while you creatures from the fields who willingly followed him are given a special invitation back to full grace. Until I can come to an understanding of this puzzle, I am a prisoner."

"Let me pose a question to you," Old Joshua said.

"What good it would do you, I cannot see," said the dragon. "But I will indulge you. Ask me your question."

Old Joshua paused for a moment, rubbing his chin as he collected his thoughts.

"Very well." He looked up at the dragon. "You seek truth, but what is your knowledge of truth?" "That is the simplest question of all," chuckled the dragon, deep within himself. "El Elyon is Truth, and I know Him."

"Yet you are not free?" Old Joshua asked.

"Fool!" the dragon roared. "Why do you toy with me? Do you want to anger me so that I eat you all on the spot?"

"I want to help you find your freedom!" Old Joshua replied.

"How can an old man like you help me?" sneered Chuian.

"If the likes of me cannot help you, then why do you waste your time riddling people, then looting then burning in rage when you cannot get your answer? You create your own paradox. You ask, and are enraged when no one can answer, yet you are convinced that one who offers help cannot deliver it," Old Joshua said.

"I do not admit that you have a point," the dragon returned. "But assuming you do, speak on."

"Oh good, I have your indulgence, thank you." Old Joshua bowed toward the dragon. "Now, most esteemed dragon, consider this. If one knows the truth, how can he rightly choose any other way and be justified?"

"Simple," the dragon replied. "He cannot."

"Very good. Now, if one knows truth in the form of being in the daily presence of El Elyon, he could not possibly be justified in turning from it to pursue his own ends. Correct?"

It was the dragon who now raised a clawed hand to scratch his chin in thought.

"I see your point," he at length responded. "Yet that answers only half my question. What of Man?"

"As you are so fond of saying, dear sir, that is a simple one." Old Joshua smiled up at the beast. "When the Anointed Cherub and his Elohim fell, they did so with full knowledge of Truth. But when Man fell, it was because he had been deceived." The dragon drew in a sharp breath. Deep lines of concentration furrowed his face as he pondered.

"You see," Old Joshua said, finally interrupting the silence, "mankind was never face to face with Truth personified. The first man heard the voice of El Elyon yet never saw Him. He had only his faith of what truth must lie within that unseen voice." Old Joshua paused.

"Go on." The dragon broke his silence. "For the first time in ages I begin to hear something."

"In short," Old Joshua continued, "El Elyon is gathering to himself a people who follow him willingly on simple, blind faith that He is. What better witness to hold before the Fallen Cherub at his judgement? What better way to show up his crime?" A rumble began deep within the dragon's chest. His grey lips began to curl back revealing glistening yellow fangs. Nikki felt the grip of fear in her stomach and was sure Joshua had finally angered the dragon beyond his point of endurance. The rumble grew to a roar as the dragon rose to his full height.

"THAT IS IT!" the creature bellowed, his voice rolling like a burst of thunder over the company, and nearly knocking them to the ground. "That is the answer to my dilemma! You have given it to me, and now I know how to choose. It is El Elyon and only Him who can be served! There is no other way!"

At that there was a terrible rending sound and the back of the dragon began to split open from head to tail. The beast fell forward across the shell of the mountain side. The company fled back to the safety of some nearby rocks, as an amazing thing took place. From where they crouched they saw a brilliant light flashing from within the dragon whose flesh was slowly beginning to melt away into a steaming, sizzling mire.

Harold huddled with the fairies. Gwydion bounded into Old Joshua's arms as he stood just behind a boulder watching the strange sight. Paul had Nikki in his arms, and both of them were also safely behind a rock. Zebedee had fled back to the little camp where they had eaten and was cowering beneath all the baggage he was able to scramble under.

From the remains of the dragon rose an amazing creature. The beast appeared to have four faces. One was like a man, one like an ox, one like an eagle and one like a lion. Each face looked to a different point of the compass. The creature gleamed like fiery bronze and from its mighty back there unfurled six golden wings which appeared to be covered with eyes. Lightning flashed about the creature and thunder pealed as the new creature rose from the remains of the dragon, to stand a full thirty feet high. The members of the company fell to the ground in fear. Nikki found she could hardly bring herself to look at the marvelous creature.

"Do not fear!" rolled a mighty voice. It was filled with power yet held in total control. "I am Eliada, a cherubim who once stood in the presence of El Elyon, and I am one of His spirits who waits before His throne to carry out His will. Rise, my friends, and have no fear!"

A sudden strength came into each member of the fellowship and they stood, all staring in amazement at the unbelievable sight before them.

"I know my form confuses you but understand that a cherubim is a pan-dimensional creature. We look quite odd when confined to being viewed in only a three dimensional context such as you behold me in.

"When the Anointed Cherub fell, and then Man followed, I could not understand such matters. I had worked so closely with the Anointed Cherub and El Elyon that my mind went dark on me and I could not see the truth. Thus was I confined to the form you beheld, and thus was I condemned to wander in confusion until I could either see the truth of El Elyon and choose Him, or slip off into the black terror of the enemy. I fear I was slipping further into that darkness this past hundred years. Your wisdom gave me the light to see that which was before me all the time.

"Know this, that I will remember you all throughout eternity and in the distant future, when these worlds are only memories, we shall have many great adventures together as fast friends. For now, however, I must return to take my place at the Throne. Yet I shall give you this aid on your quest!"

The shining cherubim clapped his mighty hands and the world seemed to explode about them in a golden flash. When everyone's eyes had cleared from the blinding light, Eliada was gone and so were the mountains. The company found itself standing in a beautiful grassy field with a great rounded mound rising before them.

CHAPTER XV

The Awakening

*F*or several days the goblin miners and sappers had been working on a tunnel directed from low on the city's hill toward the moat. The past two days had seen fighting at a minimum. Days were spent with archer attacks on the walls but always from a safe distance. The enemy lost fewer soldiers that way and so did the king.

It was easy enough for the archers on the walls to reach the enemy. The bogies had rolled up great wooden wagons which were raised into a shielded platform from which four enemy archers could stand and fire.

On the day the fellowship landed on the shores of Skye Isle, the goblin miners accomplished their goal.

"Look! What is happening?" one of the archers on the wall cried. He pointed toward the moat.

"Some more devil's magic!" cried another, as all eyes on the front wall were turned to the great whirlpool spinning just left of where the drawbridge had been. A moment later, with a roar and a mighty splash, a cascade of water spouted from the side of the hill far down toward the village. Rock, shoring timbers and a number of unlucky goblins were thrown out with the vast rush of water.

"They have tunneled into the moat!" another fairy-soldier cried. "They're draining it!"

"Look!" someone else shouted, pointing toward the forest near the village. There, from among the trees, came teams of gigantic draft beasts pulling great siege towers. The beasts looked like huge oxen and were armored in heavy iron plate barding. Ten to a team, they strained at their harnesses as behind them the great siege towers creaked and groaned forward.

For over an hour the engines rumbled their way forward, ever up the hill toward the city walls. Finally, as they drew to within range of the king's archers on the walls, a renewed assault was begun on the fairies.

The enemy archers behind the huge wooden shield wagons opened up with a barrage of fire unlike any seen since the siege was begun. Red Caps, bogies, and goblin archers advanced to take their places with those on the front lines. To the fighters within the palace it seemed that every breath drew an arrow.

"They can't keep this up for long," cried one fairy-warrior who was huddled low, like everyone else on the wall now, in a defensive posture, curled up as tightly beneath his shield as he could get. Black arrows rained in torrents.

"What makes you think they can't?" another called to the first, hoping to keep his concentration off the hail of arrows by an attempt at conversation.

"They'll run out of arrows!" called back the first. "There could not have been enough wood in the forest for much more!"

Suddenly, as if having heard the warrior's comment, the arrows stopped. Cautious heads peeked above the battlements. Ten great towers lumbered amazingly close to the city walls now. The creak and groan of the towers was accented by shouts and cracks of the whip from team masters hidden within the structures.

The towers stood three stories tall with a fighting platform surrounded by wooden palisades on the very top. The forward wall on the third level of each tower was a drawbridge, winched tightly shut.

With shouts of defiance, the fairy-warriors opened an assault on the approaching nightmares, but to little avail. Closer and closer rumbled the towers of destruction until they were only yards from the empty moat, then the teams were cut loose. The beasts bolted and ran in all directions at finding themselves freed from their burdens.

Masses of the black army began pouring in to help push behind the towers, and in spite of the hail of arrows from the city wall, slowly the towers inched forward again.

The first tower hit the side of the dry moat. The soggy earth gave way too much to one side and the great tower groaned and toppled sideways with a mighty crash. A cheer went up from atop the wall, but the second tower had already begun its attempt. It too found the soggy earth of the moat and pitched forward, smashing its topmost level into the side of the wall. The giant structure burst open, spilling its content of warriors into the mud.

In iron plate great firbolgs, and hobgoblins wielding huge double bit axes were cast about like rag dolls. They were immediately attacked by a rain of arrows from above. Scrambling for cover, some dove beneath the ruins of the tower while others attempted to rejoin those who approached in the next wave of assault.

The third and fourth towers reached the muddy moat side together and together they mired and began to pitch. As fate would have it, they pitched toward each other. The two great towers smashed against one another like the clap of a titan. One broke at its center and reeled back to upright, its top half sailing on, exposing its undefended rear to the wall. Immediately, fairy-arrows found their targets and many hobgoblins left their world with arrows in their throats.

The other tower managed to right itself following the collision, rumbling upright into the moat, and crashing against the base of the wall. An axe head smote the winch rope, and the tower's upper drawbridge rumbled down, clashing against the battlements of the wall. Hobgoblins and firbolgs swarmed out accompanied by a resounding victory cry from the black army below. Dark warriors poured into the first successful tower and up its stairs to join the fighting on the wall.

Even as the fighting on the wall began, the fifth tower crashed to its doom in the moat in the same way that its three predecessors had. Horns blared and hoarse cries from Red Cap and hobgoblin war-riors filled the air as the other towers made their attempts at the wall.

Eventually, two more successful runs were made. Out of the original ten siege towers, only three made it, but they were now a constant source of entry for the black armies below. Greatly outnumbered, the fairies began fighting their way back toward the palace wall.

Night was falling as grim-faced fairy-warriors fought with hearts set on dying in glory for their king. Fires raged within the wall's barracks, and buildings in the city streets blazed as the black hosts poured over the walls. Slowly the king's soldiers pulled back through the city and behind the walls of the palace, and the gates slammed shut, with only a few of the enemy having made it inside. Within moments the tops of ladders were seen jutting up about the wall. The enemy was about to pour over the last rampart of defense and into the palace of Gwyn ap Nudd.

✷ ✷ ✷

"I can't believe it," said Nikki, as she rubbed her hand across the smoothness of the stone slab which was set like a door into the mound before her. "After all we've been through, here we are at the very mound of the sleeping warriors."

The others of the fellowship stood quietly behind the girl.

"Reoumph!" Gwydion snarled suddenly, making Harold, who was holding the Cait Sidth, jump.

"He said, 'Open it, for heaven's sake!'" Harold interpreted.

"It is time, indeed," Old Joshua said, as he stepped up behind Nikki. He took Nikki's hands in his, giving them a reassuring squeeze. "We have come through much, but our quest is not over yet. We must now awaken the warriors and deal with the demon, Apollyon. What is before us may be harder than all we have yet come against. Are you ready?"

"I'm ready," Nikki said decisively. She smiled at the old man who had led them through so much. "Let's go in," she added, as she produced the golden key won from the kelpie.

Nikki placed the key into the small keyhole, which was the only feature on the surface of the rock slab door. The key fit perfectly. She gave it a twist but it would not budge. A look of puzzlement crossed her face as she turned back to face the company.

"The words of command!" Paul suddenly shouted. "The words True Thomas gave you, remember?"

"Of course! How dumb of me to forget something like that," Nikki said. She turned back to the door. "In the name of the Lamb, in the way of the Lion, by the power of innocent blood!" she shouted, then twisted the key. It turned easily in the lock.

A rumbling, grating noise filled the air as the door began to vibrate. Slowly, ever so slowly, the door swung inward. In a moment a rush of air burst forth with a hiss as the seal around the portal was broken. It smelt of ages long gone as it rushed past them and dissipated in the fresh outdoors. The door moved inward until soon they stood before a great gaping entrance into the side of the mound.

"It is time to go in," Old Joshua said, as the company stood staring into the darkness. "Nikki, will you lead the way?"

Without another word Nikki entered the darkness. The others followed, Paul at one side of her, Harold at the other. Old Joshua came next, carrying Gwydion, with Eilian at his right and Fionn at his left.

The inside of the mound, like inside the sithein of Ossian, was immense. It was all one great room with one hundred stone biers scattered about as if by no particular design. At the foot of each bier was a golden brazier, with a fire burning in each. By these flames was the great hall lighted.

Upon each bier was a sleeping warrior. Each was dressed for battle in the finest of armor, but none of the fearsome warriors breathed. For all intent, they looked dead.

"There!" Paul's hoarse whisper broke the silence. He pointed to a bier at the center of the room.

Within that central coffin was a warrior much larger than the others. On his right arm was a garter, and at his side was a great war horn, inlaid with silver and gold. Upon the length of the warrior, clutched in his hands, was a great two-handed sword in a jeweled sheath. The three items gleamed with magic in the dimness of the mound's twilight.

Around this bier the company gathered, all eyes on the three magic items before them. They stood silent, and almost dared not breathe for fear of spoiling the enchanted items. Finally, it was Paul who spoke again.

"Who's going to do it?" he asked.

"It should be the wizard," Eilian answered.

"That is true," Fionn joined his opinion.

"He'll have to change back into human form," Nikki said.

"No," Harold spoke. "This is a job for a warrior and Paul is the only fighter we have from the Fields of Man."

"Harold, we really need a wizard for this job," Nikki protested, but Old Joshua held up a hand to silence her.

"Ramph! Meerrrow, merph-reow!" The Cait Sidth shouted, then jumped from the boy's arms to the floor.

"Yes, as Gwydion just said, it is Paul's destiny to do this thing," the old man spoke. "The legend says, 'He who draws the sword, cuts the garter and blows the horn,' so we know it must be a man.

"It was you, Harold, who found Nikki when she was in the grip of Apollyon; you who led her to Tir Nan Og; and although you did lead us to True Thomas through his enchantments and are destined to become a great wizard of the deep magic of El Elyon, the 'He' of this legend must be a swordsman and that is Paul, our warrior from the Fields of Man."

The old man gave an encouraging nod toward Paul who then tentatively stepped up to the side of the sleeping warrior. Slowly he reached out, his fingers closing about the hilt of the great sword. When he had a firm grip with his hands he began to pull and as he did so a tremendous shudder ran through the warrior before him. Paul recoiled for a moment, then again began to pull.

With a sound like the hiss of a great snake, the sword came sliding from its scabbard. It was carved of stone and polished to a gleaming ebony. Paul fully expected to be overwhelmed by its weight, but was surprised by the lightness of the magic weapon. It yielded readily to his hands as he deftly slipped the point of its blade beneath the garter on the sleeping warrior's arm.

With a snap, the garter gave way to the touch of the sword's gleaming edge and suddenly a shudder ran through each warrior in the place. Paul felt the nerves knot up in his stomach as the great warrior before him drew in a deep breath, then expelled it in a heavy, sleepy sigh. The others of the fellowship looked quickly about them as other warriors began taking heavy breaths and giving deep yawns.

Paul nervously set the sword back at the warrior's side and reached for the gleaming war horn. Slowly he picked it up, and trembling with excitement, placed the mouthpiece to his lips.

"BA-ROOOUUU, BA-RUU BA-RUUUU!" The blast of the horn resounded with echo after echo from the stone walls of the great chamber and warriors rose up from their slumber with mighty shouts and battle cries from an age long past.

"To arms! To arms, my brothers!" the great warrior before Paul shouted, as he rose up and then sprang to stand upon the bier where he had slept for ages. "Our time is upon us! Rise up for the saving of all!"

The walls and floor seemed to shake from all the shouts and battle cries as warrior after warrior bounded to his feet. Comrades grasped one another in great bear hugs and others exchanged hearty slaps on the back as the army of sleepers came to life.

Artus, the great warrior whom Paul had awakened, then turned toward the members of the fellowship, who were huddled together in wonder. Even Old Joshua seemed impressed and Gwydion arched and spat like a Halloween cat in his excitement. Artus stooped and lifted his sword, then jumped from the bier, landing in front of the company.

"You who have awakened us," boomed his voice, "tell me what dire threat is upon the fair land."

"Apollyon is loosed!" Old Joshua answered, and at the news, the chamber went deadly silent.

"You have a dire story to tell," Artus said, in his very deep voice. He waved to his warriors to gather around as he spoke. "Through all the ages I slept,

I dreamt of mighty deeds to be done in the name of
El Elyon and His Son the Lion-Lamb, but never did
that nightmare enter my mind."

Old Joshua told their story as the warriors lis-
tened intently. When all was finally told, Artus
ordered everyone out of the mound and into the
field before it. Night had fallen while the fellowship
had been within the mound and now the moon
rode high over the land. When the entire company
of warriors and questors were gathered in the moon-
light, Artus came out and approached the fellowship.

"I have prayed to El Elyon before joining you,"
he announced, as he joined the gathering. "I now
know what we are to do." He then lifted the horn
which he wore slung over one shoulder. He sounded
a blast on it and from the distance it sounded like
thunder answering. The sound did not stop in a
moment like thunder does, however. It continued
and built in volume as it went on. Within a moment
the moonlit horizon wavered and undulated like a
snake, and the thunder-like sound increased.

"Horses!" Eilian cried. "He's called their
horses!" Great black war horses could be seen galloping across the plain toward the mound. Hooves
flashed sparks in the night as the horses charged
forward and hot breath steamed from their nostrils.

"Yes, young one," Artus said. "My warriors and I must ride to save the king, while you must call down the demon himself! You shall do battle with him on this very spot!"

As the horses thundered up to and surrounded the mound, Artus turned toward Paul and handed the great sword to him.

"It is to be you, this I was told by El Elyon, who will use the sword to destroy the evil of Apollyon!"

"But I..." Paul began, but the great warrior silenced him with an uplifted hand.

"It is to be," Artus boomed, then softer he said, "When we have ridden, read this." He produced a small scroll from his belt. "The rest will happen as it will but at this moment, kneel, boy!"

Paul knelt before Artus and the warrior drew a smaller sword which hung at his side. It was an ancient English long sword and rang like a chime as it was drawn forth. Artus touched Paul upon the shoulder with the silver blade.

"With the touch of this blade and in the name of El Elyon, I create you Knight of the Table Round," Artus proclaimed. "Rise, Sir Paul, and prepare for battle!"

Without another word Artus turned to his horse and swung up into the saddle. The mighty warriors mounted their horses. Artus nodded and his lieutenant gave a battle cry, then the warriors charged forward and to everyone's surprise, they rode the wind like solid ground and disappearing into the west.

Paul gave Old Joshua a questioning look.

"It is time," Joshua said, nodding gravely.

The boy unrolled the scroll and lifted his eyes up to the heavens.

"*Eloi eknoi Akoshnoway!*" he read in a loud voice and the heavens parted like a curtain being drawn at the opening of a play. Behind where the heavens had parted there opened the same black void Harold had faced in Rae's backyard, and from the void descended the archdemon Apollyon.

CHAPTER XVI

The Last Battle

*A*bject horror struck the hearts of the fellows as the terrible archdemon descended from the void above them. The faces of all waxed ashen at the sight of the terror from the abyss.

As the embodiment of evil touched down, the ground beneath them rippled like the skin of an animal, causing fissures to burst about them, spewing fire and brimstone into the air. Nikki, her breathing choked by the tang of sulphur, fought the terror which strove to win victory in her heart.

Before Nikki realized that she was no longer standing, and was in fact on her knees, she saw the

demon pointing and speaking to Paul. She could not make out the conversation for the roaring of the flames muddled even the booming voice of the demon. As she looked around she saw that the others of the fellowship were sprawled about upon the trembling ground.

"The sword is the road," Nikki muttered to herself. "Thomas said the sword is the road, and that it must be... PLANTED? What did he mean, what did he mean?" She knelt there muttering to herself, only half aware of her soliloquy, with her gaze fixed on the scene before her of the demon and the boy warrior.

"I can still hear him with his thick Old English accent, 'The sword is the road,' he said. 'And the lamp which outshone Antiochus...'" She paused again in thought.

"Strike me now, if you dare, you pathetic little mite!" Apollyon snarled at Paul, who stood with stone sword drawn and held at ready. "For after your best effort I shall destroy you and shall set up my master's throne on this world. Then will the Anointed Cherub reign supreme!"

The monster stood twenty feet high at least, dwarfing all about it with a body that resembled an obscene crossing of fish and man. Harold would later reflect that it reminded him of the Creature

323

from the Black Lagoon. The bloated black octopus-like head rippled like a partially filled hot air balloon. Its tentacles waved over the fanged maw from which issued sulphur and smoke as the evil phantasm spoke.

With a cry of defiance, Paul hefted the sword and raced toward the monster, and swinging the great blade he hacked into the leg of the demon. The leg severed and the creature screamed and fell backward.

"No!" it cried out, "you have slain me, child!" It dissolved in a burst of vapid green smoke.

The earth ceased to tremble and for a moment all looked at one another in stunned silence.

Then lightening struck directly in front of Paul and the thunder bowled him backward. Apollyon stood before him.

"I hope you enjoyed my little joke," the demon said, in a low sneering voice. "I know I did," it bellowed, and laughed hideously.

"In the name of Eben-ezer, there MUST be a way to defeat you," Paul rasped hoarsely, and he charged forward, again swinging the magic sword.

Energy crackled about the creature from hell as the blade sparked and flamed, slamming against a force field of some sort which had sprung up about the monster.

"HA! Try again, you puny scum!" the demon taunted. It then reached down and thumped Paul with a forefinger and the boy fell sprawling across the ground, sword flying from his hand.

Bruised and cut from his falls onto the broken, rocky ground, his chest aching from the demon's thumping blow, Paul lifted himself to his knees. He reached up and wiped the sweat and dirt from his eyes. Crawling forward, he gained the sword again.

"Oh? We're not finished yet, are we?" the demon bellowed with glee. "Ha, ha! But the boy has spunk. It's too bad spunk doesn't amount to anything in this battle, isn't it?" With that, Apollyon raised a foot and stomped the ground. The shaking earth sent Paul flying again, and the entire fellowship was scattered about by the shock. Nikki did not even know she was crying as she fell. Over and over, she repeated the words True Thomas had spoken to her at their parting, but no sense came of them.

"Don't worry, little scum," Apollyon bellowed at Paul. "I'll kill you soon, but I am so enjoying this little game, aren't you?" Sulphur fumed from the demon's maw as it bellowed its laughter.

"Now here's one I KNOW you'll like!" Apollyon shouted. The monster held its right hand out and it shimmered, then changed into a huge flash camera. "Say 'cheese,' pretty boy!" The huge camera flashed and a bolt of energy flew from it, striking at Paul's feet. The earth heaved, splitting open and Paul fell forward into the fiery fissure.

"No!" Nikki screamed, as she staggered to her feet. "That light has him blinded, he's falling!"

"Meeer-aph!" Gwydion snarled, and leapt atop a boulder next to the girl.

Apollyon leapt forward and scooped a hand into the fissure, catching Paul just before the boiling lava claimed his life. He sat the boy back on the ground.

"No, no, no, my boy," the beast mocked. "Not yet, I'm not finished with you, yet."

Cut and bleeding, haggard and worn, Paul glared up at the creature.

"I'll get you yet, Godzilla." Paul's voice was barely a whisper yet it took all the effort he could muster. "We haven't come to this point for the likes of you to win."

"Wait a minute!" A thought sparked in Nikki's mind. "That brilliant light made me think! The lamp which outshone Antichous! Eben-ezer, the Son of El-Elyon, is called the Light of the World! The lamp which outshone Antichous was the Menorah, the symbol for the Light of the World!"

"I will find a way to strike you!" Paul shouted hoarsely. "And the sword of El Elyon shall be your undoing!" With that the warrior-boy raced forward to deliver his blow.

"NO!" Nikki screamed, leaping to her feet. Paul spun in mid-run, his concentration broken by the girl's outcry.

"Don't strike him!" she shouted. "I know the answer! I know the only way to destroy him! Don't strike him!"

✻ ✻ ✻

"This is our final hour," King Gwyn ap Nudd spoke. He had gathered his ancients to the front line of warriors who faced the palace wall. Ladders were appearing along the top of the wall, and within a moment the enemy poured up onto it.

As they mounted the wall, fairy-archers picked off the bogey beasts, but they came so fast and there were so many of them that before long they were leaping successfully into the courtyards of the palace and racing to attack.

The king and his ancients had placed a magic wall of force before the fairy-warriors, but with the strength of the ancients growing weak, the magic could not hold for long. Within a few minutes the palace grounds were crawling with enemy warriors. They outnumbered the fairies three to one as they clambered and lunged at the magic force-wall which flickered yellow-green before them and separated them from their victory.

"Our barrier is giving way!" shouted one of the fairy-magicians and sure enough, holes could be seen forming in the flickering of the magic barrier. Red Caps and hobgoblins began pouring through the gaps in the magic screen and the fighting was renewed. Within a few moments the barrier disappeared entirely and the entire black army surged forward with a cry of victory.

Fighting was hand-to-hand, and the king's army was rapidly pushed back to the very steps of the palace. Many fairies fell as the dark army forged its way forward, slashing their way through the valiant warriors. Then suddenly the air was split by a resounding war horn blast.

"The Horn of Artus!" the king cried. "I know its sound. They've gotten through! Come, lads, the victory is ours!" With a great cry, the fairy-warriors fought with renewed strength, stopping the advance of the dark forces before them. Then the air was rent with a closer blast of the horn, and warriors charged across the sky above the pinnacles of the palace. Fire flashed from the hooves of the horses and the air was charged by the collective shout of the warriors. The armies on the ground stopped fighting for a moment and all looked up at the magical cavalry which rode the night sky. Then the black army turned and began to flee back toward the city wall. Great blasts of fire shot from the swords of the warriors, hitting the enemy in droves. Over and over, the mighty war horn rent the air and with each blast, strength was sapped from the evil ones until it was all they could do to crawl. Fairy-warriors pursued the enemy, cutting them down with ease and shouting, "A sword for the Lord El Elyon and for Eben-ezer!"

The army of evil bogies was scattered and fled to the four corners of the compass as the magical warriors rode the wind and the king's army poured from the city. The king's warriors charged onto the hillside, then down into the village, singing a rousing victory song, and as they fought, the sun broke over the eastern hills.

✳ ✳ ✳

"Babble on while you can, my pretty," Apollyon bellowed at Nikki. "You could not know that you have been promised me by the Anointed Cherub when this is over. Then shall I come into you and you shall bear my Nephilim children as you should have done ages ago, but you could not know that yet, could you? Our offspring shall be giants in the land as in the old days before the waters came upon your world!"

"No way, squid face!" Nikki jumped to her feet and shouted back. "I know what True Thomas was telling me. I didn't understand what he meant at first, but I do now." Nikki turned and explained to her companions. "Thomas' thick brogue made me misunderstand him. 'The sword is the ROOD,' not the road and rood is the old English for 'cross.' In my world we also know El-Elyon and in His temple of old there was a great golden lamp stand which stood for The Light of the World. Now I know who the Lion-Lamb is!"

"How can you know that!" Paul exclaimed.

"Plant the sword, Paul, it is Excaliber! Drive it back into the rock!" Nikki cried to the boy. "Plant it in the earth from which it grew, trust me!"

Paul's face lit up as realization dawned in him. He lifted the great stone sword above his head. His muscles strained as he then plunged the weapon point first into a large rock beside him.

"NO!" The monster howled in agony. "No, you can't do this. It was all planned so well! The Anointed Cherub said your people had forgotten the ancient mystery!"

As the archdemon cried out, the earth shook and the stone sword began to grow. It thrust its way upward, growing as high as the monster before it, and as the sword grew it began to change. Pulsating with a golden light, it changed into a great Celtic cross. From it branched tongues of light which formed the six branches of the lamp stand. When it had reached full height, with a mighty roar there leapt from its center the golden form of Eben-ezer — the Lion-Lamb Himself.

"My servants have defeated you in spite of all your scheming and plotting, Apollyon!" Eben-ezer roared at the monster.

"No!" the creature bellowed back. "It is a mistake! You don't understand. I was going to turn on him. I was going to undo all that the Anointed Cherub did in his rebellion! Remember how I used to serve you of old? Remember the wonderful times we once had together? I was coming back. You've got to believe me!"

"You are a liar like your father, the Devil!" Eben-ezer roared back, his eyes flashing like red fire. "Your sin is too great and you enjoy it too much. You would never come back, even if you could!"

As the fantastic beings spoke, the void above disappeared and from the sky there descended two cherubim. They held great bronze chains in their hands, chains which glowed as if they had just been drawn from a fiery furnace.

"You can't do this!" Apollyon bellowed, as the cherubim landed, one at each side. Together they bound the creature who struggled against them, to no avail.

After they had bound the monster, one of the cherubim lifted up his face and sang out a chord that resounded like the grandest pipe organ in creation. Its sound seemed to vibrate the very fabric of reality until behind Apollyon there opened a great swirling hole in the air. As the fellowship looked on in stunned silence, it swirled into infinity. It was like looking down into a tornado from the top.

"I now banish you to the pits of Tartarus until that final day of your judgement!" cried Eben-ezer. Then with a powerful bound forward, the Lion-Lamb butted the archdemon squarely in the chest with his great golden horns and Apollyon was sent reeling backward into the swirling abyss of Tartarus.

"Curse you, Nikki Renn!" the monster cried, as he fell spiraling into the abyss, growing ever smaller as he went. "I will have my revenge upon you, wait and see!"

The second cherubim then lifted up his face and another pipe organ of the universe sounded from him. The abyss closed behind them. The two blazing creatures of glory then began to ascend into the heavens, as the sun rose in the east. And as they ascended, a golden spiral staircase appeared. It lengthened with the two cherubim as they rose into the sky, finally disappearing from sight in the rosy dawn. The great golden Ram then turned and walked toward the dazed fellowship. He stopped before Nikki.

"I told you that you knew me, my child," the great ram said to the girl. His breath smelled like a field of spring flowers and his coat of golden wool held the scent of fresh-mown hay.

"Oh Eben-ezer!" Nikki cried. She ran forward and flung her arms around the golden ram's massive neck, burrowing her face in his lovely-smelling coat. "I love you!" She choked back tears of joy.

"And I love you," the ram said, "each one of you. And you will all come to live with me some day, but for now I must leave you "

"Where are you going?" Nikki asked, stepping back a bit. "Can't we all go with you?"

"I have to return to my Father's house for a little while," the ram answered. "But I will be coming back one day for good. For now, however, there is still much work to be done. There are still adventures ahead for all of you, but remember, I am always with you. Even if you can't see me I am always watching you and you will hear my voice, yes, even within the Fields of Man!"

With that the great Ram turned and began to ascend the golden staircase. As he climbed upward, the spiral stairway dissolved away beneath him. When he had climbed a way into the air he paused and looked down at the fellowship below.

"I will send you back to the palace of Gwyn ap Nudd the easy way!" he called down. He then blew toward them and he and the golden staircase vanished, but the breath of the Lion-Lamb traveled toward the fellowship, growing as it came. It rushed down and picked the company up, carrying them high into the sky.

Like a shot they flew through the sky, the land passing below them at an unbelievable speed. Within a moment's time they were over the ocean, and then before they had time to think about it, they were over land again. The land of Tir Nan Og passed beneath them in a blur, until in what seemed only moments from when they lifted off, they saw the palace of Gwyn ap Nudd coming up beneath them.

They began to slowly descend as the palace appeared and before long they were able to see the people of the Tylwyth Teg gathering below them. All were looking up in wonder and pointing, as the whirlwind carried the fellowship down and settled them in the courtyard, right at the feet of the king. He was seated on a stool on the very hillside which a short time before had been a raging battlefield.

CHAPTER XVII

Farewells And Goodbyes

*S*everal days had passed since the final battle. Nikki was in the quarters the king had assigned her, standing before a full-length mirror. She was dressed in the fairy-garments given her by Ossian and about her shoulders was a sheer blue cape which had been sent to her just this morning by the king himself. It fell from her body like a sheer blue spider's web and just touched the floor behind her. She was just fastening its golden pin when Eilian entered the room.

"Oh, it's beautiful, Nikki!" the fairy-girl exclaimed as she walked in. She wore a similar cape of gold. "I just received word and thought you would like to hear. Phadrig, True Thomas, Tom-Tit-Tot and Nonnie have just arrived and the king has called an audience with the entire fellowship. The court minstrels have even composed a song of our adventure. It is to be sung at court today. Isn't that exciting?"

"I can't wait to hear it!" Nikki exclaimed.

"I can't either," Harold's voice interrupted from the doorway. The boy stood there dressed in a sky-blue robe and hood spun of pure linen. "And don't you ever dare tell anyone back home that I wore this thing. Puss 'N Boots made me do it!" Home. At the sound of that word Nikki's heart sank for a moment. Not so long ago, when the doubt existed that she would ever see home again, she had been terrified. But today was the day that Old Joshua said they were to return to their world, and the prospect of now leaving the land of Tir Nan Og and all their magical friends made her more than a little bit sad.

"I guess we'll be going today, won't we?" she said to Eilian and Harold. "Oh Eilian, I'm going to miss you so much!" Nikki and the fairy-girl hugged.

"And I you, Nikki," Eilian said, as she drew back from their embrace. "I have a feeling that we shall meet again. But even if not, we shall be together when Eben-ezer returns to rule all worlds together as His kingdom."

"Come on, you guys," said Harold. "They're calling for us. That's why I came to get you. We are among the guests of honor." Together the three walked the golden corridors of the Great Hall of the King of Tir Nan Og.

The nobles of the land were seated about the feasting tables as Nikki, Harold and Eilian reached the Great Hall. There, at the massive doorway, they were met by Paul and the rest of the fellowship.

"I see we are all here now," Old Joshua said, as the three arrived. "Shall we go in?" They entered the great hall with a flurry of trumpets and were escorted to the high table of the king. There was a seat for each member. Even Gwydion, still the Cait Sidth, had a scarlet pillow placed on the table itself for him to sit on. The old wizard-cat did not seem to mind this at all. He leapt upon the pillow, turned round and round several times, then settled comfortably onto it.

Phadrig sat on his haunches at the table; he was also upon a scarlet pillow. There was even a place of honor in the corner near the king's table for Zebedee the pony to stand.

When all were in their places, the king rose to his feet and lifted his golden drinking horn high.

"I propose a toast to the fellowship of the Sword, the Horn and the Garter!" the king called out.

"To the fellowship!" The entire company of the great hall answered the toast.

"It is my understanding that the young Harold is to grow in the ways of the deep magic of El Elyon, and to do so under the guidance of Gwydion ab Mathonwy. Therefore, I decree that the east tower of the palace central be singled out as his. It is to be stocked with all the best books in hopes that he may find the need to cross over again into the land of Tir Nan Og!"

Ossian stood and now raised a toast following the king's words. The king nodded in response to Ossian's toast and lifted his drinking horn.

"To Harold the Blue!" The cry rang out about the great hall. Harold felt his face flush.

"Reoumph!" Gwydion snarled next to the boy.

"Don't worry," Harold returned. "I'm not getting a big head."

The king then turned from the table and walked to his throne, which sat on a dias just behind him.

There he took up a sword and turned to face the audience again.

"I command Fionn and Eilian to come and kneel before me," the King called, and the two fairies left high table to obey.

"I do commend you for your courage and bravery in the quest, and I do now create you peers of the realm." The King then placed his sword upon the shoulder of Fionn, and then Eilian.

"Arise, Sir Fionn and Dame Eilian! From now on you shall have a place at high table with me."

Another toast was called out, this time to the new peers of the realm.

Sir Fionn and Dame Eilian returned to their places. Then the king called Nikki and Paul.

"Nikki Renn and Sir Paul Martin," the king addressed them as they came to him. "You are examples of the best that the Fields of Man have to offer. You shall return to your land with the blessing of Elfame upon you. There you will find that old age flees from you and as the years pass you by, youth will cling to you. So it is with those who have become kindred souls with the land of Tir Nan Og."

Again a toast was called out and the cheer rose from those at the tables about the great hall. "It will also be good to know that once again a knight of the table round walks the Fields of Man," the king added, with a smile.

Next the king spoke of the years of service that Old Joshua, Gwydion, True Thomas, Phadrig and the others had rendered and each were given high praise and commendation from him and were pronounced personal friends of the king. Even Zebedee was decreed a royal pony, and that he should never carry a pack or burden again.

After all the announcements, the king called for his chief minstrel to come forth and render the song of the fellowship for the court, and then the feasting went on for long hours. Time and again the song was called for until nearly everyone present had learned it and could carry it back to their individual sitheins. Then at last, the revelry broke up and everyone began to go off to whatever business they had about the palace. Old Joshua called the fellowship together in his chambers and when everyone was present, he began to speak.

"My friends, we have traveled far and been through much together," he said. "Now it is time for goodbyes."

At this, Nikki's heart sank. Going home was the one thing she had wanted more than anything at all through the adventure, but she had not in those times been thinking of the parting of friends.

"Do we have to go now?" she asked. "Can't we stay for a while? Eilian says time does not flow here as it does back home. What would it hurt if we stayed?"

"That is the danger for Children-of-Man in these fields," Old Joshua said. "You would stay and play and frolic and before you knew it, centuries would have passed in your world. No, we must have you off today, right now as a matter of fact."

"Reomph?" Gwydion meowed.

"No, my friend," Old Joshua returned. "I am not going back, at least not yet. There is something strange in the air and I cannot for the life of me figure out what it is I am feeling. I am going to stay and do some casting about. Perhaps it is just the imagination of an old man."

"Merph!" Gwydion returned.

"Oh, I've thought of that," Joshua answered. "Thomas, Gwydion is asking how he is going to keep an eye on these charges of his all by himself. Will you agree to go back in my place to help him? You could say that you are my cousin, and live in my house."

"I would be honored to do so," True Thomas returned. "It has been many a century since I have seen the fields where I was born. It will be interesting to see the wonders these Children have spoken of."

"Then that settles it," Old Joshua said. "Are you all ready?"

"Wait a minute," Nikki called out. "Before we go back there is just one thing I want to do while we are still in Elfame — that is if you will agree to let me."

Three days later the entire company stood in the midst of the forest Andramear. Joshua and Gwydion had agreed to Nikki's request and Phadrig had also consented.

"There he is," the great Phouka said to Nikki, as he indicated a huge spreading gold-leafed sycamore tree. It stood noble and proud, deep within the Andramear, and with a tear in her eye, Nikki slowly approached the beautiful tree as the company looked on in silence. The girl stepped up to the golden tree and reached out a tentative hand to stroke its bark. At her touch the tree gave a small shudder which caused its golden leaves to rustle lightly overhead. She then placed her arms around the great trunk and hugged it tightly.

"Oh, Willie," she cried, "I'm so sorry that I didn't know how to take good enough care of you when you lived as a kitten in my world. I'm sorry you got run over! You were the very best kitten anyone could ever have and I will always love you!"

A greater shudder ran the height of the golden tree. Its leaves began to rustle again, only this time much louder than the first. The sound grew until it sounded as if a great wind was stirring the Andramear, yet no breeze blew in the forest. Then suddenly, the golden leaves began to come loose from their stems and fall. Within moments, Nikki and the company were showered with thousands of big golden sycamore leaves. The golden cascade continued until every leaf on the tree was turned loose. Then a deep sigh was heard coming from the tree and the golden aura which shines from the trees of the Andramear faded from the sycamore.

Quietly, Phadrig padded up to Nikki who now stood a few feet from the tree, ankle deep in golden leaves. "Your words brought him great comfort," the Phouka said. "He has found the strength to pass into the heavens where he will assume his duties as one of the fiery spirits which wait upon El Elyon day and night. You have done a good thing, Nikki."

"It is time," Old Joshua said, from behind Nikki. Last hugs and goodbyes were exchanged between the fairy-folk of the fellowship and the Children, and everyone promised to try to meet again one day. Then Old Joshua called Nikki, Paul, Harold, Gwydion and Thomas together in a circle.

"Everyone join hands," he commanded, then he said, "*Eloi Keyos-ney prush-niotie Key-onyotie!*"

The world flashed green and the forest floor seemed to fall from beneath their feet. Nikki felt herself falling but it was not a scary feeling. In the distance she could hear beautiful music, as if a great choir were singing a very lovely song. It gave her a warm feeling all through her spirit. Then a flash of blue-white dazzled her.

"Oh, that was bright!" Nikki exclaimed. Her vision began to clear and she saw Paul standing before her, next to his camera and tripod. She was wearing a very sleek and trim purple one-piece bathing suit and standing before the backdrop in the Martin living room.

"Hey, you guys." Paul's mother stepped through the archway from the hall into the living room. "Are you going to slave away at that camera all day? I've got some sandwiches made in here if you have time to take a break."

Nikki grinned at Paul. The boy smiled back and turned to face his mother.

"Hi, Mom!" he chirped happily.

His mom shook her head and grinned. "Love struck, that's you two," she said, laughing. "From the silly grins on your faces a body would think you'd been up to some adventure this morning."

"Mom," Paul returned, "You don't know the half of it." The two chuckled at their private joke as Mrs. Martin shook her head in amusement and went ahead of them to the kitchen.

"Oh, Paul, look!" Nikki stooped and picked up something at her feet. She lifted it gently in her cupped hands and Paul stepped forward to have a closer look. Nikki held a single sycamore leaf, still gleaming with the golden light of Elfame.

THE END

Coming next: Swept to a time hundreds of years before the flood of Noah, Nikki and Harold find adventure "Beneath a Mirrored Sky."

LARRY C. HEDRICK

I decided when I was fifteen-years-old that I wanted to be a writer. Everyone told me that I would never be able to do such a thing, so I did it. Along the way, I managed to finish high school, go to college for about a thousand years — mounting up credits but never graduating, go to seminary and graduate with a divinity degree, work in the religious field for one lifetime, become a newspaper reporter for another lifetime, and now I am a novelist.

Throughout my school, I wrote short stories but never attempted to have anything published due to the fact that my parents insisted that such a feat was impossible, feeling that writing is close akin to magic and "normal" people are not able to do such magic. Through the decade of the seventies, I actually attempted getting published and found that it was impossible because writing is something close akin to magic and "normal" people are not able to do such!

In 1980, a newspaper editor read some book reviews I had written and decided he wanted to hire me, thus began my career as a writer. There I wrote the news in a style that my city editor, John, described as being closely related to a detective novel. I also wrote a weekly entertainment column for the paper, which I enjoyed to its fullest. It was at that time that I began the first chapter of this bok, ten year prior to its publication.

There are to be at least two more books in this *Beyond the Shores of Time* Series, with Nikki and company. The next is *Beneath a Mirrored Sky* and the third title changes daily. There are also several other projects planned aside from the saga of Nikki, Harold, Paul and the others, but those are tales for other days.

It is very fortunate for me that I married Sonya Elaine Clay, just over five years ago. She is the greatest wife a person could ever have, a top-notch editor, and the greatest restaurant manager in the business. She has worked hard these past years to keep us from starving, while I worked exclusively on my writing. As yet, we have had no children but we have a black cat named Phadrig, who allows us to live with him!

For a FREE catalog
write, phone or fax:
TOP OF THE MOUNTAIN PUBLISHING
11701 S. Belcher Road, Suite #123
Largo, Florida 34643-5117 USA
Fax: (813) 536-3681
Phone: (813) 530-0110